WERE-EAGLES DARE

The Silencers Series

Whip Lipsey

Etherege & Wycherley

Cover design by: Kristi Date-Lipsey
Library of Congress Control Number: 2022909317
Printed in the United States of America

WERE-EAGLES DARE

A full moon lights the grounds of an abbey. A gusting wind drives dust against granite walls. In the distance, lightening flashes and thunder faintly rolls. Dull yellow light shines through the windows of a stone building, vaguely Gothic, but built by masons not even vaguely Gothic themselves. The building stands two squat stories; not monstrous, but capable of holding monsters. The light from the windows shines out on cobblestones upon which no feet tread.

Inside, the building houses a laboratory, vast and cluttered with beakers on tables and shelves. Not new, modern, well-marked beakers, but more like your grandfather's beakers. Cloudy bottles of yellow and green, used absinthe bottles, skull and cross-bone bottles. Nothing from which you'd care to receive liquid. Past the bottles, along the walls, stands electrical gear in a fashion reminiscent of the nineteen-fifties and clearly not ready to pass a safety inspection: an old autoclave, a large bottle-spinner sized for your grandfather's beakers, a toaster surrounded by crumbs.

In the main room lies a large wooden examining table, set at a forty-five-degree angle, to which great iron manacles are attached by great iron links of chain. Attached to these lies a man. He is Otto, but not for long.

Otto sounds concerned, "Herr Doctor?" Mid-twenties, skinny, blonde, and pale as a ghost, Otto's only notable feature, other than being chained to an antique table, is the black tattoo of a swastika covering the whole of his pallid and sallow chest.

Otto sounds increasingly concerned, "Herr Doctor

Damarung?" Otto watches a needle withdrawing from an arm.

That arm belongs to Count Frederick von Orlok. He says, "Thank you Herr Doctor. As always, I am revitalized." Orlok is a tall and stately middle-aged man; silver haired, lithe of limb. He speaks slowly, Germanically, but a purring sort of Germanic. He gestures with great deliberation. He moves with studied care. He chooses his words with precision and grace. Yet all his words sound grimly mocking. You could imagine him as General Rosemeyer in *Where Eagles Dare*, or even better as Count von Krolock in *The Fearless Vampire Killers*. Either way you would be imagining the actor Ferdy Mayne. See that man, and hear that voice, and you have Count Orlok.

At the other end of the needle, wielding it like a practiced jouster: *Herr Doctor,* Doctor Damarung. He is squat, flat headed, wears thick glasses, and for all the world appears as if the mad off-spring of Jean Paul Sartre and Peter Lorrie.

Orlok wears beautifully tailored, slightly purple, formal wear, reminiscent of an earlier age; even earlier than any you now imagine. Say, maybe, 1755, but toned down a bit, with fewer frills on the shirt he now rolls down, and a less elaborate coat than the one he now puts on. Doctor Damarung wears a white lab coat of an old bib-shirt style, buttons running down the left and right. Though no less of another age, he does not share that age with Orlok.

Now wearing his full regalia, Orlok looks to the table upon which Otto lies. He slowly, gracefully approaches the back of the examining table. Otto cannot see this, as the table faces away from the approaching Count Orlok, but Otto can sense his approaching presence. Orlok, after all, doesn't leave *presence* to chance. He practices it nightly. Orlok arrives at the table, standing beside it. Even on the tilted table, Otto 's head still lies below Orlok's. Orlok raises his hand and places it at the top of the table's edge as he languorously rounds the table to face Otto. Count Orlok does everything with languor.

If he is not sardonic, then he is languorous, or both at once, and that's just Orlok.

Otto notices the Count, but Otto does not give the impression that he thinks that he is now *rescued*. He sounds nervous, "Ah! Herr Count Orlok! Such an honor." Orlok reaches his hand down from the table edge and strokes the side of Otto's head as one might do to a kitten—before drowning it. Orlok smiles. The least reassuring smile in the history of amused expression.

Orlok offers a small tribute, "Otto. My Otto. I so appreciate that you have volunteered." Otto throws a smile at Orlok, a smile that might best be called "desperate" but that will probably be recalled as "heroic."

Otto rambles a bit, "Yes! Volunteered! Anything for the Brotherhood! All together in love of our destiny and a curse on our enemies!" Otto begins to recite his catechism, "I am oath and honor bound to do all in my power to further the Brotherhood in fulfillment of the perfect vessel for the Final Resolution of our great cause."

Orlok purses his lips and shakes his head just slightly. It is so unnecessary for Otto to express his earnest commitment at this stage.

Doctor Damarung steps into Otto's line of sight. Damarung's look and manner contrast perfectly to Orlok's. Not only short and squat, but graceless and abrupt in his every gesture. Damarung fiddles with vials and test tubes on a side table, and you can feel the vials and tubes cringing at every sharp move of the good Doctor's pudgy fingers. Damarung spins to face Orlok, a move that by itself would scare a small child, and when he addresses the Count he speaks with such clipped phrases that each word seems to attack its colleges in their shared sentence, "Now is our moment. We must strike. Let us use the Beast in the Cell!" He says it just like that, capital letters.

At this Otto begins to lose composure, or what he still has where he once had composure, "Ah! Ohh! Ah!"

Orlok puts a soothing hand on Otto's chest, "No. No." Orlok shakes his head reassuringly. "No. That won't be necessary." Otto calms, looking more reassured than a man chained to an antique dissection table has any right to.

Doctor Damarung spoils Otto's mood, "Why not? An experiment. If we are to have a suitable vessel when the brothers arrive. Why not? Let us start our great work!"

Orlok raises a hand to ward off another recitation of first principles and gives the slightest tsk-tsk shake of his head. "We must first clear the way," Orlok gestures sagely with his hand, in the manner of an ancient high priest, "we must walk ... before we may run."

Otto could not agree more. He nods his head with a vigor almost sufficient to free it from its chain.

Doctor Damarung presses on, "Even so. If we must," he nearly strangles the words as they leave his mouth, "clear the way ... then why not use The Beast? We have it already prepared."

Orlok cuts him off, "No. We need something more controlled. More ... directed." Orlok turns to Otto. "You understand what you must do. Draw blood! Make them pay for their presumption. Show no mercy. Tear them to pieces."

Otto nods in hearty agreement, "I am ready!"

Shuffling sounds emerge from behind Doctor Damarung. Orlok comforts Otto, "Not yet. But soon."

Karl von Hapen enters the room with a hairy-man, the later with a chain around his neck and lashed to a pole held by Karl. The hairy-man wears blue dungarees and a blue button-down shirt. Karl wears uniform black, SS officer uniform black in fact. Karl himself is a yellow haired blonde and as pale as Otto. Indeed, of those present only Orlok sports a mild tan. Hair covers the face of the hairy-man, so who knows?

Face covered in hair. Not just a beard and side-burns. It grows profusely up to his eyes, on his neck, on his hands, even his fingers. His buttoned-up shirt puffs in a manner suggesting hair beneath. One might expect to see him in a circus.

But not, as it were, *on the moor*. Which is to say that he looks not in the least fearsome. Short, thin, stooped and wary, you might pity him, but you would not fear him.

Still, the pole-and-chain restraint.

Orlok notices the arrival of Karl, "Ah yes. Karl. Bearing our *means of instigation*." Doctor Damarung sniffs in disgust and fetches a sealed vial from the side table.

Karl brightens at being addressed by the Count, "I brought the liveliest one, hoping it would help."

Damarung snorts, "Of these, one as bad as another."

Otto tries to assert some control here, "I'm ready to go now, Count Orlok. I'm ready for my mission."

Orlok waves him off, languorously, "A moment, Otto." To Damarung, Orlok asks, "You have the scent extract?"

Damarung responds, "The barest whiff will do."

Karl smiles. His thick lips are genetically predisposed to curl cruelly, but Karl has improved on nature, and we will always see him practicing this particular art.

Otto says, "I will crush our great enemies completely!"

Orlok nods, "I'm sure you will."

Karl brings the hairy-man closer to Doctor Damarung and to Otto, keeping himself at the opposite end of the pole.

Otto offers a helpful suggestion, "If you could unchain me ... and we could talk of weapons."

"Oh no, Otto," Orlok says, "*you* will be the weapon."

Orlok backs away from Otto. Doctor Damarung opens the vial for just the briefest moment beneath the hairy-man's nose. The hairy-man sniffs the air. Twice. His face contorts. The body of the hairy-man jerks. It jerks again. It seems to stretch. The hairy-man shakes and twitches.

Orlok steps back from the table, "Herr Doctor, be so kind as to aid Karl in securing the fiend."

Doctor Damarung grabs the pole. Together he and Karl guide the increasingly agitated man-beast toward the chained and panicking Otto. Orlok directs them, "Gently. Gently. Just the barest bite."

The hairy-man transforms before our eyes. His fingers grow to resemble claws, his face becomes something of a muzzle. His teeth grow into fangs. Thus transformed, he still does not resemble something you would call out the whole village over, but you would arm yourself with a pitchfork against him.

Otto screams, "No! No! No!" The hairy-man-beast rages and strains at his leash. He catches sight of Otto, helpless on the table. No need to lead him now, he lunges viciously at the helpless Otto.

Karl shouts, "Hold him! Hold him!"

Orlok, instructs calmly, "Ease him to our champion."

Otto offers a different opinion, "No! Stop! No! Please!" But *please* has no magic. In an instant the hairy-man-beast lands upon Otto, gripping Otto's leg in his horrid teeth. Otto screams, "Arrrrggggghhhhh!!!"

Doctor Damarung yells at Karl, "Back it off!"

Orlok concurs, "Retract the fiend."

Karl and Doctor Damarung pull the hairy-man-beast away from Otto. Otto's screams subside. He struggles to see his wounded leg.

The aggression of the hairy-man-beast wanes. His muzzle becomes a face again. His claws become hands. Hair drifts to the floor, leaving him only very hairy once more. The hairy-man-beast becomes, again, just a strangely hairy-man.

An unnatural calm falls over the lab.

Karl relaxes his grip on the pole-and-chain. Damarung releases his grip altogether. The hairy-man whimpers and strains on his leash away from the chained man he had a moment ago attacked. Doctor Damarung and Karl look at Otto, chained and wounded. Damarung with a look of clinical concentration, Karl with one of sadistic anticipation.

For his part, Otto looks calmer. It really seems a minor wound after all.

Behind Otto, Count Orlok backs slowly away from the table. Seeing the scene from where Count Orlok stands: before us the table, obscuring Otto still chained on the incline facing Karl and Damarung. Beyond the table those two, staring intently at the table. Beyond them, his leash now on the floor, dropped even by Karl, the hairy-man cringes at the lab door from which he entered. Orlok watches the back of the table as Otto addresses them in the stillness of the lab, silent but for the sound of the wind outside.

"I think I'll be alright. Really just a scratch. I feel fine."

Then, still from Orlok's view, we see the table shake. We hear banging from the table. It rattles violently.

Orlok demurs, "Oh no, Otto. You will be so much more than ... all right."

Now a succession of bangs and rattles emerges from the table. Beyond the table we see Karl's eyes go wide. We would doubtless see the same from Damarung's eyes if we could see them through his thick glasses. Or perhaps we wouldn't, maybe he sees this sort of thing all the time.

A hand lunges out from the table into Orlok's view. Not a hand, more a claw.

Orlok smiles. "Karl. Take hold of our glorious instrument. Lead it to the place of intrusion. Let the work of this night commence." Karl smiles cruelly, as he is apt to do, and detaches the leash from the hairy-man. Orlok watches with contentment and triumph. Doctor Damarung's expression might better be described as: demented joy.

At the Cohen farm – night

At the foothills of the Andes, night embraces a small farm. It must look a pleasant place at other times. In the light of day the mountains would rise in majesty, or at least to impressive height, and fields would reveal their bounty. It has the look of a place tended with care and competency. Vines from a vineyard give way to a small hedge, beyond which lies a low roofed barn. Across the way a modest house.

But this night casts the farm in a sinister aspect. Moon shadows turn the vines into tangles. The wind blows strong. Lightning flashes in the distance. The alpacas look jittery. Perhaps the wind has them on edge. Or maybe something else.

Perhaps the sound of teeth ripping flesh. Behind the hedge a werewolf eats an alpaca. This time a proper werewolf. Not a hairy-man briefly *wereish*, but a convincingly frightening wolf-man, all black and gray fur, but for a white fur swastika splashed across its chest. Clearly you need to call out the village on this one.

It chews its fresh alpaca meat while looking over the small hedge row for a better meal. And such a meal now walks into view. We see her walking from the barn carrying two full pails of fresh milk. Young, pretty in a farm-hardened way, modestly dressed in work clothes and handling the large pails with ease, it is Hadassah Cohen. The wolf-man sees her as well, a more satisfying helpless victim than the alpaca.

The wolf-man begins to stalk her. Slowly it covers the ground between them, the noise of its movements concealed by the sound of the wind. The wolf-man eyes its victim with the pleasure of easy dominance over the helpless. Hadassah pauses, sensing something. The wolf-man pauses with what one could call relish.

The wolf-man gathers itself over its powerful legs ready to spring. Its victim looks around in the chilling wind, unaware of the night's terror. The wolf-man springs at Hadassah. In mid-air a pail, still half full of milk, crashes into the wolf-man's head. The wolf-man hits the ground. It shakes off the blow and searches for its victim.

It sees Hadassah, still holding one pail of milk. The wolf-man rears up. It displays its full were-beast might, swastika in plain view of its victim, and lets out a powerful howl. "Ooooooou-uuuuhhhh!!!!"

A milk-pail hits it square in the jaw.

The wolf-man shakes off the blow and scans for its prey.

Hadassah runs full tilt for the barn. The wolf-man takes off in pursuit. It closes the distance between them. Hadassah appears to trip and fall to the ground. The wolf-man rears up for the final pounce.

A digging hoe hits the wolf-man square in the forehead. The wolf-man yelps and leaps back.

Before the wolf-man stands Hadassah, armed with a digging hoe, and looking a good deal less terrified than an attacking werewolf might have hoped. The wolf-man looks its victim straight in her eyes and snarls. She looks back with an expression one might read as ready-to-hit-you-in-the-head-again. Wolf-man meet Hadassah: place *helpless* at one end of the globe and you will find her at the other.

Suddenly, behind the wolf-man, a yellow light shines from a door to the house across the small yard. A voice sounds from the newly opened door. "Hadassah?" The voice comes from Hadassah's brother Ehud Cohen. He has a young, lean, farm-hardened physique. Clean shaven and clean cut, he wears functional farm clothes and a yarmulke. He steps from the door looking about. "Hadassah?"

Hadassah shouts, "Wolfen!"

The wolf-man tears off toward Ehud, a black form in the night, approach covered by the wind. Ehud scans the darkness. The wolf-man leaps at Ehud.

Ehud rolls backwards beneath the wolf-man, kicking its body over him, using the werewolf's momentum against it. The wolf-man flies in the air landing hard on the house porch in front of the door. The wolf-man rights itself and looks out at the yard, seeing the unarmed Ehud helpless before it. It growls and readies another pounce when—damn it!—another blow to the head!

This one from behind, delivered by Hadassah's and Ehud's brother, Ezra Cohen. Ezra is the shorter, broader, curly-haired compliment to Ehud. He holds a baseball bat. More accurately, he swings a baseball bat at the now retreating wolf-man.

Retreating, but not defeated. The wolf-man swats at Ezra's bat and has another go at Ehud. Hadassah shouts, "Ehud!" She throws her hoe to Ehud who catches it and hits the wolf-man with a glancing shot. The wolf-man turns to attack Hadassah and is struck with a rock right between the eyes. It sees Hadassah rearing back with another rock and retreats toward the barn wall, roaring. The three Cohens form a phalanx. They back the wolf-man up to the barn wall. It paws angrily at the air between them.

Its back against the wall, the wolf-man looks at the sight before it: three Cohen siblings, Hadassah with rocks, Ehud with a hoe, Ezra with a bat. Then, joining them, carrying a spear with point gleaming in the moonlight, the large and bearded form of Amram (Papa) Cohen. Papa Cohen looks like a Rabbinic power lifter. Arms like oak limbs.

Now the wolf-man knows it is in trouble. It growls and roars and gathers itself to leap over the battle-line of Cohens. As it leaps, Papa Cohen lunges with the spear, catching the wolf-man in mid-leap and pinning it to the ground with a mighty blow. Still holding the spear pressed down into the wolf-man, Papa Cohen turns to his offspring. With a ferocious Conquest of Canaan gleam in his eyes and a voice from the Book of Judges he declares: "That's how you do it, Kinder! Put the pointy end straight through the swastika!"

Looking down they see the wolf-man pinned to the ground by the spear. With its last breath it unleashes a howl of despair. "Ahhhhhoooooooo!!" As it does so it transforms. Becoming a man again; small, pale, his shed hair blowing away in the wind. Transformed from wolf-man back into Otto. Poor Otto, impaled on a spear.

Within the Abbey library – night

From a tall arched window framed in stone we see lightening flashing in the distance and hear the wind blow. The wind carries in the distant howl of a wolf, a forlorn call. Peering out the window, which rises high above him, stands

Count Orlok. "A howl of victory?"

Behind him, the hunched and squat form of Doctor Damarung answers, "I fear not."

The howl fades.

Orlok turns from the window, "Alas." He raises his hand in a benediction. "In memoriam to fallen champions." Perhaps something can break Orlok's reservoir of studied indifference, but it won't be the death of Otto. "Well. The living must carry on." As Orlok draws away from the window we can inspect the room. Before us we see what once served as a monastic scriptorium, built in stone in high medieval style. It serves now as the library and study of Count Orlok, and it displays the man. Tall spire-like windows rise on either side of a giant fireplace that once warmed the frozen hands of scribes; or would have warmed them had the building actually been built at a time when men copied manuscripts by hand.

The surrounding walls of granite suggest an architect worried about Viking invasion, or, in the event, impressed by such anxious architecture. These walls would serve against a ballista and could keep the Huns at bay, should the need arise. A man could copy the whole of the works of Augustine and make a good scratch at Boethius with nary a glance of concern out its tall windows.

But while its originators may have wished to harken back to the Middle Ages, it has since been converted to a warmer glow, even if not to a contemporary aspect. Tapestries and paintings fill the walls, none more noticeable than that over the fireplace. Here rests the charming rococo painting *Portrait of Mademoiselle Guimard as Terpsichore* by Jacques-Louis David. Mademoiselle Guimard, dressed in soft teal and pink, bonnet and all, steps lively over an arrow wielding cupid amongst the flowers, seemingly oblivious to the threat of falling into the faux-medieval fireplace above which she frolics.

Around her, tapestries show hunting scenes or tableau of

classical myths rendered in eighteenth century iconography. Books proliferate, beautifully bound and placed on antique shelves. On the floor, surrounded by so much art, rest sofas, divans, and tables filled with a museum's worth of objects d'art. Every item in the room, excepting Doctor Damarung, could be precisely dated somewhere between 1715 and 1788. Count Orlok has made the room to mirror its inhabitant; it reflects back to him just what he wishes to see of himself.

Orlok addresses Damarung, "I would have preferred the removal of our … embarrassment … before the arrival of the brethren."

Damarung replies, "We still could—"

"No. We will simply need to work around the problem."

"But after. Then we can—"

Orlok waves his hand, "Yes. Of course. In our own good time. When our gathering has concluded. When the brethren have departed."

Damarung, "And our great business complete."

Orlok, "Yes. When we have completed our business. Business must come first."

Orlok inspects his room, "And *then* our pleasures."

The Silencers

Against such villainy what can the world offer? From Interpol at least, it offers *The Silencers*. Natasha, the precision weapon. Rafe, the fast-talking trickster. Trevor, the gentleman cat-burglar. Kip, artificer and tech-whiz. And Marcy Gainer, creator and curator of Interpol's answer to the question: Who can we send that's expendable? *The Silencers*. Que our theme song: *Rock Fort Rock* by the Skatalites.

Within an old bus – Argentina – morning

A beautiful summer's day at the foothills of the Andes. The *Neumatico Desinflado* bus company serves this road. One could describe their buses as: *authentic.* A particularly authentic specimen makes its way, swaying a bit on the rough road, uphill. Very up hill. It carries mostly rural folk; farmers, herders, and vintners of the rugged Andean Mountain region. They look well-kept and chat amiably with each other, mostly in Spanish.

Among them three stand out, tourists, though they blend well. They are Marcy Gainer, Assistant Supervisor of *Interpol Task Force 13 (Confidential)* (aka: *The Silencers*). She travels incognito, that is, dressed for hiking in the mild but changeable weather of the lower Andes, with her husband Chris Gainer, perennial graduate student in anthropology and full-time father, and his charge, their daughter Katrina Gainer, two and a half years old and a precocious talker. Katrina holds her usual place, Daddy's lap, in her usual manner, standing. She plays with the six-year-old girl sitting across the aisle. Marcy occupies the window seat. She tries to write on envelopes, but the bumpy ride frustrates her effort.

Little Katrina talks to the six-year-old girl, "Good rattle. Rattle rattle."

The girl shakes the rattle at Katrina.

Chris Gainer talks to his wife, "What do you so miserably fail to write?"

Marcy, "Briefing papers."

Chris, "I thought we left Halftrain a thousand miles away."

The girl tells Katrina, "Para ti." She gives the rattle to Katrina.

Katrina, "My rattle?" The girl nods.

To her husband Marcy says, "I left the Grand High Pontiff of Dependency to his own devises. He assured me he could handle all business without me. He did that while shredding the Investigation Division's payroll checks, so leaving room for doubt. But when I offered to get the department ahead on reports and briefings, he gave me a lecture on motherhood and how in the old days Interpol only hired unmarried ladies and spinsters as secretaries. So I just left him there, with his tie caught in the shredder. Hopefully, Halftrain won't bring down the free-world in my absence; or he'll at least be saved by some random spinster still wandering the building from 1952."

Chris, "Harsh but fair."

Katrina shakes the rattle.

Chris to Katrina, "Say *gracias*" Katrina giggles. To Marcy he says, "So whom do you brief?"

Katrina yells, "Grassy butt!" The girl laughs.

Marcy mock frowns, "Cultural expansion indeed. I'm sending notes to the team." She displays her scribbled on postcards. "Rafe and Natasha are stuck at Headquarters. So these should find them without trouble. I'm supposing Interpol Communications Division can forward on the others to Kip and Trevor wherever they are."

Little Katrina broaches her favorite subject to her generous new friend, "Candy?"

Chris, "Katrina!" The girl giggles. He sighs, "At least say *dulce*."

A game try: "Duckly?"

"Lo siento."

Katrina may not speak Spanish, but she knows when candy has been denied. Marcy puts away her papers. She takes Katrina. A diplomatic woman by nature, she looks to head off any international incidents. To Chris, Marcy says, "I promised you a working vacation where you get to work while I vacation. So I'll manage the Little Hellion; you learn local culture." Katrina stares out the window at the ever-rising terrain. "Assuming she will stop jumping back into your lap."

"Child-laden or lap-barren I appreciate your planning all this just for me. I know we must put your career first, so for you to take vacation time to follow me on research means a lot. And to find such an interesting place as well."

For one so fulsomely praised Marcy looks just a hint uncomfortable. To Katrina she says, "Say *Argentina*. Say *Argentina*."

Chris, "That's too many syllables for her."

Katrina, "Argentina!"

Marcy laughs, "I think someone came into this world to make Daddy look foolish."

The bus pulls to a stop. The driver announces, "Pueblo de Seguridad." The riders make for the exit.

Chris, "Is this the place?"

Marcy, "One town before." The girl waves goodbye.

Marcy calls out to the bus driver, "Driver, we are going on to Nido de Aquila."

Everyone on the bus freezes. The driver looks like someone just asked to be dropped off over a cliff.

Katrina, "Uh oh."

Marcy wonders if *going on* sounds like some unsuspected Argentine curse, "The station master said to request it at the end of the line."

The remaining passengers, all on their feet, begin murmuring "no" and "por favor" and "pobre condenada." Marcy doesn't speak much Spanish but understands that the general consensus argues against her request.

The driver pleads, "No. No."

Marcy, "We'll pay any additional fee." Marcy holds up some local currency. With that the bus community gives up trying to save her. No one can reason with North Americans once they start waving money around. The locals exit the bus. The bus driver drops sullenly into his seat and heads further up the road.

Chris, "Not exactly heartening."

On the streets of Nido de Aquila – Argentina – day

The bus pulls up, the door opens, and out comes Chris, carrying Katrina. At the door of the bus, Marcy offers cash to the driver, but he waves it off with a pitying look. She exits, and the bus pulls out with what those in the bus driving profession refer to as *unseemly haste*. The Gainers take a gander at the village of Nido de Aquila, and it looks ...

normal. Quiet. Oddly German, but without gargoyles or goblins of any sort.

Chris, "Given the hub-bub I expected something a bit more menacing."

Marcy, "Lethally threatening, to go by local opinion down in the valley."

Little Katrina, "Scary place no-no."

Chris and Marcy hoist backpacks onto their shoulders and head into town. Katrina walks between them. The town looks like a quaint Argentine village as imagined by a Bavarian who had never traveled beyond the Alps. The rising mountain backdrop might tempt anyone into placing an Alpine village here, and the local planning committee succumbed. The buildings conform perfectly to the ideal of pre-war rural German town architecture; Idstein in the Andes. Katrina suspects the houses are made of gingerbread and licorice. Chris must restrain her from licking every window frame.

What people they see adds to the effect. Big-boned pale blondes wearing clothes best described as *lederhosen-derivative*. The villagers nod politely as the Gainers pass, with just a hint of suspicion. The Gainers make their way. They walk beneath a clock tower, pride of the village no doubt.

Open-minded anthropologist though he is, Chris finds the town just a little hard to get. "What country did you pick for us again?"

Marcy sees his point, "A bad case of Old-World envy."

"The un-melted German remnant of the Argentine melting pot."

A pair of older ladies pass them, dressed appropriate for the Andean summer. Marcy smiles and addresses them as Chris tries to teach Katrina architectural terms like *dormers*.

"Hola. Me puede decir el terror de las Montanas?" The women look at her for a moment in shock, then hurry away.

Chris points to a quaint shop among the quaint shops,

"You wanted new postcards?" They head toward the shop. Marcy engages another passerby as Chris enters, "Hola senior. Me puede decir el terror de las Montanas, por favor?" His mouth gaps open for a moment. He hurries off.

Inside the village stationer, Marcy picks out four postcards while Chris inspects the store shelves and keeps Katrina close at hand among the breakables. It will not do to have one's child smashing knickknacks in a foreign language. Chris walks Katrina through a sea of German themed kitsch. How could such a small town, so far off the main tourist line, support so great an industry in Teutonic bric-a-brac? And what is a *Kehlsteinhausdorf* that it should be so frequently printed on everything from key chains (a major typographical challenge) to Nutcrackers?

Chris notes a ceramic eagle in the Kaiser Wilhelm style. Next to it a ceramic mountain monastery titled *Kloster Adler*. He picks up a little Kehlsteinhausdorf clock tower like the one they passed in the town center. He sees Katrina likewise inspecting an item. He bends down, "No honey, don't play with the—" swastika?

Chris picks up the little porcelain piece, oddly elaborated with bars through its central legs, these ending in a circle at its center. None the less, a swastika. He returns it to its shelf of tiny swastika table-toppers. He takes his Kehlsteinhausdorf clock tower to the cashier, a middle-aged, beer-rounded man with white hair. The man has just finished his transaction with Marcy. Marcy asks her now standard question, "Por favor, me puede decir el terror de las Montanas?" The store owner looks at her quizzically.

Chris, "Try German."

"Right. Bitte, Was ist der Terror in den Bergen?"

The store owner's face drops, then rises again in anger. He slams the register shut and points to the door. He tells them, "Geschlossen! Closed! Closed!" Chris puts the Kehlsteinhausdorf tower on the counter and they leave.

On the street again Chris hoists Katrina up. To Marcy he

says, "Impeccable German."

Marcy looks about, distracted and searching for more people to query, "I studied up before the trip."

"But you brought us to Argentina, so why—" Before he can finish, Katrina has detected a likely port of call.

"Candy! Candy! I want candy! Please." She points to a shop bearing the sign *Schokolade*, a testament to the town's tourist economy—in spite of containing, by all appearances, just three tourists—and to Katrina's sweets-based foreign language vocabulary. They head over to the candy shop.

Inside the shop the Gainers view a display of chocolate and sugar sufficient to rend a pediatric dentist to tears. Chris manages Katrina's selection process, by way of a liberal use of the hated phrase "just a few," while Marcy waits for the shop-keeper to appear from the room behind the counter. With some difficulty, and without attempting an adequate explanation, Chris manages to ward Katrina away from the swastika themed gingerbread cookies, the Wehrmacht helmet hard-candies, and the Iron Cross licorice sticks. Thus properly guided, Katrina picks a last piece for the candy bag, delighted at her haul. Chris carries her to the counter where Marcy addresses the cashier.

"Bitte, Was ist—"

Chris interrupts, "Wait." Chris pays for Katrina's candy and then motions for Marcy to proceed.

"Bitte, Was ist der Terror in den Bergen?" You could knock the cashier over with a Feder. He slams the register and holds Marcy down with a glare. The Gainers leave.

They stand outside, Katrina content with her candy, Marcy scanning for more interviewees. A pair of women start to pass. Marcy steps up to them, "Por favor, uh bitte. Wo kann Ich finden die Cohens?" The women hurry away, almost in a panic.

Chris, "You certainly have a way with the locals."

Marcy, "I wish we had Rafe here. He'd know how to get some information from these people."

Within an Interpol interrogation room – Washington, D.C.

You may think you have seen interrogation rooms before, but no interrogation room you have seen, in film, on television, or on your more unfortunate afternoons, looks so much like an interrogation room as this one. The key: keep it simple: A bland room, to forestall distraction; a table, for the placing of incriminating documents; a hanging fixture with a single light bulb, because someone wants to uphold inquisitional traditions.

Seated before the table, and clearly the man under interrogation, we find Rafe Riley, man of confidence. You might even call him a confidence man. Ruggedly handsome with a smile you can trust, if you are the sort to trust in smiles. If you are not that sort, Rafe can talk a line of patter to keep you just one step ahead of suspicion and two steps behind comprehension.

Rafe will, apparently, need that skill here as he faces Mr. Abel and Mr. Yates, each holding documents, presumably incriminating. Rafe looks confident. More so than usual, and he usually looks very confident.

Mr. Abel speaks first, reading from a report. "Rafe Riley." He looks at Rafe accusingly, "Where did you get a name like that?"

Mr. Yates, "The man wants to know the location of your name."

Rafe talks as if to a microphone hidden it the light bulb, "Can we get some coffee in here? Tea?" To his interrogators he says, "You boys look tired already. Have some coffee." Rafe motions at the lightbulb, "Order some donuts if you like." Yates looks up at the light, baffled.

Abel, "You're the donut pal." Abel gestures to Yates, "He's the hole. And I'm your worst nightmare."

Yates offers, "Don't mess with the hole. You mess with the hole you get the..." Yates stumbles, but in his defense "hole" does not give you a lot to work with.

Abel slams a paper onto the desk in front of Rafe, "Eyewitness testimony, and it gives you up."

Rafe leans over the document and appears to read it: "I heartily recommend the exceptional agent Rafe Riley for promotion beginning October eleven. He is the most extraordinary agent since Halftrain."

Abel snatches the document from the table and examines it, momentarily dumbfounded. Then he reads it aloud, "I hereby swear that I saw Rafe Riley, on the night of October eleven, take documents from the safe of Supervisor Halftrain." Abel slams the document down before Rafe. Rafe scrutinizes it like a Kabbalist seeking secrets in the Torah.

Rafe shakes his head and points at the document to read each word as he indicates it. We can see Rafe's finger under each word in turn as Rafe reads each slowly. The words are: *I hereby swear that I saw Rafe Riley, on the night of October eleven, take documents from the safe of Supervisor Halftrain.* Rafe reads it as: "I heartily recommend the exceptional agent Rafe Riley for promotion beginning October eleven. He is the most extraordinary agent since Halftrain."

Abel snatches the document up again and squints at it.

Yates slams down a document, "You stole these documents from Halftrain's safe!" In bold letters at the head of the paper: TOP SECRET.

Rafe reads, "Tickle Susan?" Rafe points twice at the page to indicate a careful finger read.

Abel starts laying out pictures before Rafe. Rafe sees a picture of a man smiling in an improbably appropriate deerstalker cap, another man wearing an artist's beret, a sultry looking woman with dark hair and wearing an overcoat while standing before the Kremlin, and a picture of Marcy, whom we so recently met. We will soon enough meet the others as well.

Abel, "Your accomplices. We mean to roll them up too."

Rafe takes the picture of the sultry woman and shows it to Abel, "When you go to capture her, film it, I'd really like to see that."

Yates collects the pictures while Abel lists on his fingers the varied evidence against Rafe, "Eyewitness, fingerprints on the safe, video of the crime."

Yates throws in, "And the paper says Top Secret, not Tickle Susan!"

Abel glares at Yates. Rafe nods approvingly, "Fine boys. But what about the secret formula? What was I supposed to do? With the lives of everyone on the planet at hazard?"

Abel, "What secret formula?"

Rafe, "The one in Halftrain's safe. The one he stole from China to unleash on the world."

Abel and Yates look legitimately baffled. Yates has a go, "Don't try and confuse us."

Rafe, "I would never do that to you fellows. You two suffer from what psychologists call *situational confusion*. It arises from the very structure of events. No one really to blame; the context alone has done you in." Possibly true, that claim. On the other hand, the context does not sit under the sweat-light, Rafe does.

Abel, "We want a confession, Riley."

Rafe, "Fine. But I want a deal."

Abel, "What deal?"

Rafe, "Two years minimum security, and I spill. Remember, that without me, you'll never find the body."

Abel, "What body!?!"

Rafe leans back confidently, "Halftrain's body. Buried in a field. And I know who did it."

Yates, "Who?"

Rafe points to Abel, "He did."

Yates looks at Abel in wonder.

Rafe yells to Yates, "Grab him!"

Then the lights go up. The real lights, well above the hanging one. A voice announces: "Good exercise gentlemen. Break for lunch."

Everyone relaxes. Rafe stands and walks around the table.

The back of his windbreaker reads: TRAINER. Rafe plays the old veteran, "And that's how it's done boys. They call it resisting interrogation, but really, it's about flipping the script. Use the clues your interrogators drop and construct a plausible story. Put them on the wrong foot and keep them there. Like wrestling an anaconda."

Abel and Yates do not look convinced. Rafe carries on, "Or at least confuse the hell out of them. Remember, the longer you keep the enemy talking, the more you delay the rough stuff. Nobody likes the rough stuff."

In a dark alley – night

In a dark alley, in the dead of night, a woman walks. Gorgeous to look at, dark hair, curvy but athletic, dressed in a black form-fitting body suit with a gray, long, split-sided jacket. Rafe earlier identified her as the woman whose attempted capture he wished to see.

She is Natasha Raskalitkanof, product of the latest iteration of the Russian Clandestine Services, but to be honest, really the product of fifteen hundred years of Russian nihilism and a general inability to get along with other peoples. Russian Intelligence recruited her young, trained her well, then lost her to the West. She has given up her Russian nationality, but not her profession. She walks the alley with a slow grace. Not the grace of a trained super model on a familiar fashion runway, but the grace of a woman who does not fear dark alleys. Dark alleys fear her.

Above her, on a window ledge, we can see, but she cannot: an urban ninja. He looks like any other ninja, the ninja dress code being fairly well settled. They hate it when people call the outfit "black pajamas," but absent the relevant Japanese technical vocabulary, what else suffices as a description? Even their split toed black shoes look just a little too much like the foot pads of a child's night-time onesie. Medieval Japanese Ninja Masters, quite sensibly, dressed for comfort. How could they know such a commitment would lead their deadly assassin uniform to resemble a child's nightwear? These men were night-stalkers, not prophets. At least they had the sense not to add a button butt-flap. Tempting though this must have been at the time. But we digress.

The ninja, hovering above in his black pajamas, watches as Natasha passes below. At the perfect moment—his ninja senses no doubt tingling—he tosses himself down upon his prey. Natasha leaps back at the last instant, leaving the ninja to bounce painfully off the pavement. Poor ninja.

Natasha might be in the clear if ninjas came only singularly, but they come in groups. Ninjas Two and Three drop from above, careful now not to try and drop *on* Natasha. Natasha notes that they do not bounce off the ground in agony. She says, "Better dropping." As a rule, she doesn't say much, but when she says something, she says it in a thick accent one might classify as *Russian Sultry*.

The ninjas attack—the least one might expect of them—launching an impressive ninjutsu joint offensive. This proves an unfortunate mistake. Natasha parries the kick of Ninja Two, sweeping his leg from beneath him, sending him to the ground. She blocks the punches of Ninja Three and cracks him karate style in the throat. As she does this, she offers commentary. "Slow."

Ninja One, recovered from his hard fall, tries a very un-ninja like football tackle, but Natasha splays her legs and sends and elbow into the back of his neck. "Foolish."

Ninja Three pops back to his feet and returns to a ninjutsu pose only to receive a foot in his groin and an elbow to his chin. He won't be jumping up again and will likely disappoint his wife for a week or two at least. Ninja Two sets for a second attack, nervously guarding his groin and keeping his chin tucked. His absurd defensive dance ends when Natasha knocks him out with a roundhouse kick.

Ninja One, barely back on his feet, pleads—rather against the code of the Dark Ninja Arts—as Natasha advances. "Wait, it's only—" What it only is will itself have to wait. Natasha beats him down with three left hooks. Natasha may have many sins, but no one has ever accused her of hesitation. The best way to fight Natasha Raskalitkanof is to *start* with surrender. You won't get the opportunity later on.

Natasha walks past the groaning ninja bodies to a doorway at the end of the alley. The sign above the door reads, *Do Not Enter.*

She enters.

Within the warehouse

Natasha walks through a warehouse space that has been decked out as an urban obstacle course; fake buildings with real doors. Barrels and trashcans provide cover points for obstacle course enemies. Boarded up windows conceal obstacle course snipers. A set decorator waiting for a break-out job in Hollywood has added a layer of urbane grit to the course. The Interpol handbook calls this reality-training, but given that Interpol's officially licensed number of armed agents comes to all of none, the course actually substitutes office cubicle SWAT fantasy for reality. Interpol *reality* revolves around not getting your tie caught in the shredder.

Natasha draws a semi-automatic side-arm and walks the course. A cardboard granny pops out. Natasha lets her live. She walks by the granny and pushes the target back into place. She walks on.

A cardboard bank robber pops out, moneybags in hand, cardboard pistol raised. Natasha lets off three rounds. One to the head, two to the groin. Red paint, but still rather disrespectful to hard working cardboard. Natasha kicks the target to the ground and walks on.

Out pops another cardboard friend-or-foe. This one in the image of a tweedy Englishman daintily holding a cup of tea. This picture bears the likeness of Trevor Sinjun-Tunsby, earlier shown to Rafe in a deerstalker cap. We will meet him later. Natasha raises her gun but does not fire. She gently pushes the image of Trevor back into place as she passes.

Natasha passes a doorway as a cardboard mugger, hands up in exaggerated *grab you* pose, pops out at her. She pistol-whips the figure, knocking its head off. She kicks its cardboard groin away for good measure. No murderous cardboard offspring for him.

Ahead of her another cardboard figure pops out. A jaunty young man holding a pair of paint brushes and a sculptor's chisel. He still wears the artist's beret Rafe saw him pictured in while under interrogation. He is Kip Carson, and we will meet him later as well. Natasha does not fire at the Kip figure. She pushes it back into place.

A figure of Marcy Gainer pops out, looking harried and carrying an armload of papers. Natasha spares her.

Then out pops a cardboard man extending a friendly hand: Rafe Riley, he of the earlier scene. This Rafe smiles beguilingly. Natasha empties her weapon center-mass leaving a tight little red-paint cluster right on the heart. The lights come up. A voice from a loudspeaker announces: "All right. Good exercise. Let's all thank Agent Natasha Raskalitkanof for the demonstration."

Trainees congratulate and thank Natasha. Wounded ninjas give her a respectful, distant, nod. A fellow trainer approaches, "Excellent demo. But why did you shoot your teammate?"

Natasha says only, "Bad history there."

At a party – a great hall – Salzburg – night

A great hall. One of the best. It takes up the better part of a lavish mansion in Salzburg, Austria and contains a party in full swing. A classy soirée hosted by Victor von Richter. He stands near the entry, greeting new arrivals and sending them on their way into the grand room.

His home's great hall contains a grand piano, a full bar, and antique chairs along the wall, their delicately embroidered upholstery below portraits of von Richters past. Another wall boasts the stuffed head of a large boar, presumably not a von Richter, though you can see some resemblance. From the center ceiling hangs a great chandelier above rugs from the eighteenth century. Above the rugs, below the chandelier, spilling crumbs on the former and casting wary glances at the later, von Richter's many guests have lively conversations in fancy dress while seizing hors d'oeuvres and Champaign from caterer's trays. A quartet plays Mozart.

Von Richter smiles and chats as guests flit past. Between such chit chat he watches the entry to the great hall, as if waiting for someone.

And someone in the great hall watches him.

The art of disguise turns on the craft of remaining incognito, but our spy looks distinctly *cognito*. Below long curly hair and a Lucifer level goatee one can still make out the face of Kip Carson. Normally a picture of innocent earnestness and prone to turning to every passing distraction, his face now sets fast on von Richter.

From Kip's vantage point we see von Richter walk to the entryway of the great hall. Von Richter meets a man in a dark trench coat and gray fedora just as the man enters. The man in the fedora makes a sign with his hands: his index finger on his chin, his middle finger against his thumb forming a bird-beak, the other two fingers stuck up, pinky under the ring finger. It goes by in a flash. As does von Richter's response: index finger on the temple, middle finger touching the cheek, ring and pinky fingers press the thumb forming a downward facing bird-beak. The two men then exchange a few words and depart together.

Kip smiles. The look of a man, or absurdist devil-man, satisfied with his discovery. He runs his eyes over the many party guests until they fall upon...

Trevor Sinjun-Tunsby. Looking even more English than his cardboard cut-out, he wears formal wear not out of place at a 1930s English country house. He talks with two attractive young ladies in a manner entirely identical to the voice and accent of the actor Terry-Thomas, premier performer of upper-class British toffs and the role model for Trevor right down to the moustache and gap-toothed smile. If you don't know Terry-Thomas, look him up on YouTube now, and you will hear Trevor's voice exact.

Trevor speaks to his clutch of admirers, "Yes, well, it is frightfully important to have the saddle and riding crop match. And of course, the proper color coordination of that ensemble with the chapeau and pantaloons, quite essential." His admirers titter at his wit. "And one's boots. It is difficult to stress sufficiently," but Trevor tries, "how the cut of one's boots effects every aspect of the ride."

The admirers look at him attentively. One asks, in a French accent, "But how do you stay on the horse?"

Trevor answers, "With a good deal of effort and a firm grip I'd say!" They all laugh. "A firm grip!"

From behind Trevor, Kip approaches. To complete his fright wig and demon-beard look, Kip has dressed himself in ruffles and lace with a coat that Sgt. Pepper long ago rejected as too garish for the Lonely-Hearts Club Band. Well draped for circa 1968, here amongst the contemporary glitterati he displays a conspicuous aesthetic to say the least.

Trevor laughs on, "A firm grip with the legs!"

Kip hesitates to interrupt, but only a little, "Lord Beaverbrook. If I may."

Trevor looks to Kip with some reluctance, "Sorry?"

Kip tries again, "Lord Beaverbrook."

Trevor offers his hand, "Well, awfully glad to meet you Beaverbrook."

Kip contains his impatience. He declines Trevor's hand by motioning at Trevor with his own as if to say: no, you. "Lord. Beaverbrook. If I may speak with you."

Trevor remembers an important part of their briefing, "Oh, of course. *I'm* Lord Beaverbrook." To the ladies, "So many titles." To Kip, "What do you want my good man, I'm engaged with Mademoiselle Touché and Fraulein ... ?

The Fraulein offers: "Fuchs."

Trevor smiles most wistfully. In his defense he rarely commands this much attention from the Frauleins. "Ah yes. The fox hunt." They laugh.

Except for Kip, "Your lordship, a word in private."

Trevor can't take his eyes off his company. Nothing pleases Trevor so much as being admired for his Englishness. Barely glancing at Kip he says, "Explain yourself, briefly, good fellow."

Not an easy task. But Kip tries, "I must in form-u la..." Here Kip's creativity fails him. "X-ray omega extreme extraction." Slipping into pig Latin he tries, "The anlay ithway ormulafay at the airstay." Kip punctuates this with a double nod towards the entry.

Now at least Kip has Trevor's attention, "Good god man, have you suffered a head injury?"

Giving up on subtle codes, Kip takes Trevor by the arm and leads him away with a nod to the admirers, "Ladies." Kip walks Trevor until they are alone in the crowd of the party. They speak in hushed tones to each other.

Kip, "Someone has lost focus."

Trevor, "I'll have you know I was gathering valuable intelligence there."

Kip, "Well, good. Adding the floozy intellect to your own, maybe you can at least remember your alias."

Trevor, "Floozies indeed. Ladies of the best breeding I'll have you know."

Kip faces Trevor and lowers his voice, "The man in the gray fedora just arrived and went upstairs with von Richter."

Trevor still searches for an unattached mademoiselle to impress with foxhunt humor, "Von Richter?"

Kip speaks slowly so the words get through, "The host of the party surrounding us to which we are uninvited guests."

Trevor, now attentive, "The man in the gray fedora you say? Did he have a package? Papers? Envelope? Anything?"

Kip, "I don't know. But they went upstairs. Together."

Trevor, "Right. A likely place for a safe, and I'm just the cracksman for it. Follow me."

Now with purpose Trevor heads to the entry. Kip sighs and starts to follow when a drunk young woman approaches. She slurs out a question, "Are you an artist? You look like an artist."

Kip answers, "Why yes I am."

She, "I love an artist. Do you paint?"

Kip, "In a manner of speaking. I don't dabble in *mere* paint. I don't apply pigment to canvass. I am in fact my own canvass. I create—" Kip gestures so as to encompass himself head to foot, "On myself, a persona that reflects itself, as a personal reality, referring that reflection of the world back upon that very self to which it owes its own existence. An existence whose artificiality my art makes real, in the fictive sense."

She doesn't get it, but groupies don't really care about the art, "I love an artist."

Kip smiles at her. Love of art. What a great party. Trevor grabs him by the arm and jerks him back to reality and towards the entry.

They make their way upstairs, pretending to be engrossed in conversation when anyone looks at them, or engaged in admiring connoisseurship of the wall art. Or, as it happens, Trevor tries to look engrossed in conversation while Kip tries, and fails, to look impressed with the stairway art. The combination looks distinctly suspicious, but von Richter provided an open bar, so absolutely no one pays the least attention to them.

Trevor, "So Bunny Brisbane lofts a wild antic up the old spout, as they say, causing a nucleic reaction among the assembled that quite undid the violent remanent of vaporous jolly containment responses, all very showy to be sure." And so on.

In response Kip looks over a Gainsborough hanging on the wall of the stairway, barely containing his gag reflex and saying things like, "Hum."

By such means the two men make their concentratedly casual way up the stairs.

Finally, Kip and Trevor stand outside the private study of von Richter, the sounds of the party below still barely audible. Kip opens the door with caution and looks into the room, Trevor behind him. The room's lights are out, and only the light from the hallway streaming in from the door cuts the dark. Von Richter has decorated the room just as one would expect from a European sophisticate. Lots of paintings on the walls; any might hide a safe. Kip looks the room over as Trevor impatiently waits behind him. Kip looks low as if trying to see beneath the furniture. Sometimes Trevor cannot fathom what wanders through the head of his partner.

Trevor whispers, "What are you looking for?"

Kip, "The Gay Astronaut."

Trevor pushes past him, "Not that bloody nonsense again."

Kip, "They send those warnings for a reason."

Trevor, "Sheer balderdash. Search for the safe, not some mysterious homosexual flight lefftenant.

Kip, "Safe's easy."

Trevor stalks the room looking about, "Far from it. Takes a keen, trained eye to see the signs of a wall safe. Could be behind anything. Spend the better part of the night searching for it." As he says this we see behind him as he walks: a frame on hinges swung open to reveal a wall safe. Kip points to it, and Trevor turns toward safe. Trevor leaps back when he sees it just past his shoulder. Trevor gathers his wits, "Amateur's fortune."

Trevor begins to work his magic on the safe. He presses his ears against it, turning its dial, listening as it gives up its secrets. He coaxes it into compliance as the safe's dial emits soft clicks. He smiles, "Behold the work of a Master Cracksman." Trevor opens the safe and looks in. A sound fills the air; gas releasing. A puff of vapor blows into Trevor's face. Trevor's eyes cross and he passes out.

Kip watches, shocked, "Gas!" Trevor, unconscious on the floor, is in no position to appreciate this less than timely revelation. Fortunately, Kip is a strapping young man accustomed to quick, improvised action. Kip covers his face with a ruffle from his shirt—functional after all—and grabs documents from the safe. He hauls Trevor up onto his shoulders and carries him out, pausing occasionally on the stairs to pretend to admire the Gainsborough and offer small talk to the man he carries unconscious on his shoulder.

Several people note Kip's behavior, but they pay no attention. Given the open bar, one can only expect this sort of thing.

The Cohen farm – day – Andean foothills

The modest and comfortable home of the Cohen's. In case it has not yet come through, the tasteful but unequivocal decor of the home shows they are Jewish. No Old-World masters here, just a framed picture of Theodor Herzl, and an elegant but simple Star of David containing words in Hebrew ("Cunning will watch over you, discernment will keep you, to save you from a way of evil, from a man who speaks perversely." – Proverbs 2:11-12.)

In this room Chris sits in a group with Hadassah and Miriam. Miriam is the wife of Amram and the mother of the Cohen siblings. She has a kindly face lined by many smiles and much work in the sun. Very near to Chris and the women, Marcy sits with the men, across from Papa Cohen behind whom stand Ehud and Ezra. Katrina stands in the "women's group" playing with a few toys on the floor, brought from a back shelf and not seen since Hadassah ran these floors when Katrina's age. Katrina busies herself redistributing the toys between the adults in her circle while the women coo over her.

Hadassah observes the obvious of Katrina, "So pretty."

Miriam says, "And so generous."

Chris, accustomed to toddler socialism, takes no notice of Katrina. He questions the women, "So rather like reverse Zionists?"

Hadassah says, "We go where we like, and we live as Jews."

Miriam urges politeness on her, "Not with foreign guests Hadassah."

Chris says, "I'm just fascinated by cultures."

Katrina knows this word, "Daddy likes culture."

They laugh. Hadassah speaks to Katrina, "I'm Hadassah." Hadassah points to herself.

Katrina points back, "Hadassah. Miriam." She gets it right. Pointing and naming is very last month for Katrina.

In the seats nearby, almost at elbows with the women, the menfolk talk menfolk things: Marcy Gainer makes a rather obvious point to Papa Cohen, "You seem unpopular in the village."

Papa Cohen responds with another obvious point, "Jews have a right to be anywhere in the world. Just like anyone else." He speaks with a Yiddish accent and a strong voice. "We love Israel. Two sons I have in the Israeli Defense Forces right now. Ehud, Ezra, and Hadassah have all done their service."

Katrina tries out some new vocabulary for her new friend Hadassah, "Terror in den Bergen." Marcy grimaces, but Chris looks slightly vindicated. Hadassah smiles wanly.

To Marcy, Papa Cohen says, "We notified your people so you should know, we did not ask for help."

Chris speaks up, "No worries Rabbi Cohen, we're not here to help. We're on vacation."

To Papa Cohen, Marcy says, "Americans call it a working vacation. A little work, a little vacation."

To himself—but loud enough—Chris says, "Yep. And everyone does the same job as at home." Like a punctuation mark Katrina crawls into Chris's lap.

Marcy tries to regain control of the conversation, "I'm not

in contact with Interpol now, but I will make a report," she glances at Chris, "if I think of it." She asks Papa Cohen, "Can I see where the attack occurred?"

Papa Cohen nods and rises, "Of course." He leads them out to the courtyard and then to the farmyard.

The bright light of day gives an innocent look to the farm, offering no hint of the sinister. Papa Cohen shows them around. The small vineyard, the modest fields, the barn with two cows. Marcy accompanies Papa Cohen. Chris carries Katrina, walking behind them.

Papa Cohen tells Marcy, "And the alpacas over there. Three of them in the last month."

Marcy, "But you don't know what killed them?"

Papa Cohen, "That would be difficult to say."

Chris wanders off with Katrina to explore a bit on his own nearby. Ever the anthropologist, he searches for the family graveyard. He sees it, fenced in and well-tended. No weeds grow on a Cohen grave.

Near the hedge row Marcy presses her questions on Papa Cohen, "Was it a more alpaca-centered attack, or were other animals attacked as well?"

Papa Cohen, "Sheep too."

Marcy, "And the other local farmers?"

Papa Cohen, "They have stories as well."

Looking about Chris sees a mound of earth well outside the family graveyard. You don't need to be an anthropologist to see that it marks a burial. Chris notices that fresh earth covers the grave. The mound has barely settled. Katrina pats the ground as if to tamp it down.

Marcy continues questioning Papa Cohen at the hedges, "Can we visit other families? I would like to talk to the other farmers about what they suffered."

Papa Cohen, "I will take you. They all know me; I am their Rabbi. But maybe only some things they will tell you." Then he whispers, "The authorities are not on our side."

Above the fresh earth of the grave rests a tombstone; in

the shape of a cross. In the middle of the fresh dirt mound, struck fast into the fresh grave, rises a pole.

Or is it a spear?

Marcy, at the hedge rows, looks off at the farmlands out in the valley. She notices a mountain top nearby with a collection of buildings enclosed by a wall. "That's the Kloster Adler?"

Papa Cohen nods, but he does not follow her gaze.

The monastery looks so picturesque one might suspect it had been added just for the tourism benefits. Marcy says, "The postcard says it's a Carthusian monastery. They must have a great view of the valley from there. Perhaps they've seen something."

Papa Cohen sounds very definite on this one point, "We have no friends at the abbey."

Interpol briefing room – Washington, D.C. – morning

A proper briefing room. A large table, suitable for holding important papers and photos off the floor. It stands in front of a map of the world from which dangles a pointer attached to a note saying: "Do Not Remove From Briefing Room!" In front of the table sit two chairs, occupied by two people. Rafe sits in one chair, in the other, Natasha. It would be inaccurate to say that they give the impression of right now enjoying each other's company. Disastrously inaccurate.

Natasha will not look at him, "Do not blame me. You made misunderstanding."

Rafe tries to return her non-look, with mixed success, "It was a date."

Natasha, "Date: a place on the calendar."

Rafe, "Date: a romantic rendezvous."

Natasha, "What is this *rendezvous*?"

Rafe, "We Americans define it as an event in which one does not assault a violin player."

Natasha, "That was misunderstanding."

Silence.

Natasha, "This *romantic*. Also misunderstanding."

Rafe, "Clearly."

Silence.

Natasha, "I am not accustomed to every American custom."

Rafe, sighing, "Taking a woman's hand, on a date, in America, land of the free, counts as typical behavior. You can reject the overture, but you don't need to arm-lock the man who makes it. Your date."

Natasha, "I made my point."

Rafe, "Use your words! Leave your prepositions out if you must, but *tell*! Verbal telling!"

Silence. A lot of it. More than that even.

Natasha, "I apologize. I felt panic."

Rafe, "You? Panic?"

Natasha, "It was unfamiliar sensation."

Rafe thinks on this a moment, "Wait. What was the sensation? The panic or what you felt when I took your hand?"

Before Natasha must answer, or return to pointed silence, Mr. Lester C. Halftrain, supervisor of *Interpol Task Force 13 (Confidential)*, and possibly the dumbest man on the planet, enters the room. He precisely resembles the manager you knew would go far at the company from which you could not get far enough away. He is the manager who takes credit for your work but thinks he has stolen credit from the idiot in the next office, until he "realizes" he actually thought of it all himself. And then he walks through a sliding glass door. And somehow still doesn't get a scratch on him. And receives a promotion for *smashing through barriers*. Meet Lester Halftrain.

Halftrain, "Gentlemen." He checks the room; only the three of them in it. He corrects himself, "Ladies."

Halftrain sits. His best trick. He gestures over his left shoulder, "My assistant Mrs. Marcy Gainer and I come here to brief you on your mission." Halftrain notices Rafe and

35

Natasha's perplexed looks. He glances over his left shoulder and smiles, "My apologies." He gestures over his right shoulder, "My assistant Mrs. Gainer."

Rafe and Natasha nod approvingly at the empty space behind Halftrain's right shoulder. They must, or they will never get out of here.

Halftrain checks his papers, "You, the members of Intriguing Pollution Flask Torch 31," he leans forward to impart a secret, "Conflicted." Here he gestures to each member of the team as he reads of the names, even to the members not present. "Trevor Sinjun-Tunsby, Kip Carson, Rafe Riley, and Not-Stash Racks-Like-Take-Off." Natasha suppresses the urge to kill. Rafe clears his throat bringing Halftrain's head up from the paper.

Halftrain checks the room. His quick finger count shows he has only two briefees. He makes a quick finger count of the names on his paper. It is a wonder he does not count on his fingers. After a bit of shuffling he finds another paper.

Halftrain, "Ah. Two of you have already left on another assignment. Tevler Sink-jam and Cart Tipster currently..." He leans forward to impart the secret information, "Seek the Secreted Formica of Exotic Oxen." Halftrain assumes that he has impressed them with this cryptic information.

In fact, Rafe and Natasha just look bored and annoyed.

Halftrain pushes on, "But *your* mission." He shuffles papers. His special talent. He does it without looking. Which is either particularly impressive or especially exasperating, depending upon which side of the desk you sit on. "I wrote these briefings myself." He gestures over his left shoulder, "Giving Mrs. Gainer a bit of a break—new mother and all." Halftrain finds the paper. "Here," he clears his throat, "Marcy Gainer has gone missing!"

Rafe and Natasha bolt upright. He has their attention now. But he makes no use of it. He just sits there, looking at them very satisfied with himself.

Rafe, "Marcy has gone missing?"

Halftrain, "She has?" He looks to his left and then to his right. No Marcy. "My God man! You're right!" Halftrain starts to slowly look in every corner of the room. "Where do you suppose she could have got to?" He looks pleadingly at Rafe, "She was just here a moment ago."

Rafe tries to take control of the situation and forestall panic, whether his own or Halftrain's he can't be sure. Rafe suggests, "Perhaps if you just read the briefing paper."

Halftrain remains concerned by the recent occurrence of either invisibility or teleportation, but he picks up the briefing paper and reads, "Missing: Mrs. Gainer out to sea, overboard. Search for the fourth richest man in Palacia regarding travails in customs and dookies." He looks around, and carries on reading, "Out to sea, continue to look for over-blown penile restitution using device of Dr. Damarung by medicating Mrs. Gainer." Here he looks up and adds emphasis with a jabbing finger, "Must stop Dr. Damarung at the coast!" Having properly emphasized this, he drives home to his conclusion, reading: "Nasty desiccated asthmatics hosting Klaus Attler with Agent Nina. Seek and find damaged/medicated Mrs. Gainer here." Then he adds, almost as an afterthought, still reading his paper, "The opera uses old cape routine with bonus arias."

Halftrain hands the paper over to Rafe, looking rather pleased with himself, "I must say, you ladies have your work cut out for you."

Rafe takes the paper and suppresses his look of confusion. He knows questions will only serve to further misguide. Oh for the good old days before coded communications. Back when everyone understood each other.

Letters – 1873-1889

From: Brother Alphonse Rodriguez, La Safforona Italy, January 15, 1873.

To: Bernard Forster, Director of the German People's League

Dear Herr Forster,

Please accept my apologies for this tardy reply to your most intriguing offer. We Carthusians, being a brotherhood founded on silence, allow ourselves only one day each three weeks to written communication least our communion with Christ suffer neglect. It has, in fact, taken some time just to speak among ourselves concerning your organization's offer to fund our proposed hermitage in Argentina, for the greater glory of God. Cleary, in our dire straits, God has sent you as an angel of mercy. Nevertheless, we should like to make a few matters clear before accepting your generous offer.

Firstly, we are unsure what sort of "German Colony" you mean to found around our proposed monastery. While the plans you forwarded look wonderful, we are an order of strict seclusion and so can have no intercourse with such a community. Nor do we quite understand what you mean by a "new founding of the German Fatherland." Of course we raise no objections to this, though we must stress that in the eyes of our brotherhood all peoples are equal in Christ.

Secondly, while we agree completely with some of your organization's sentiments, we remain puzzled by others you mentioned in your letter. We heartily agree on the need for "social discipline," "respect for tradition," and "absolute obedience." Music to our ears, as they say. (To be clear, we Carthusians, in fact, ban all music.) And of course we also hate the Jews. We do feel the need to stress, at least this once, that the Jews are to be loathed as Christ-killers who rejected the Savior and stole the word of God from the Lord's own lips. We, as a secluded order, are not up to date on the "latest scientific racial thinking," as you put it, but surely it is unnecessary to assure you that there are no Jews among us. We are all good Catholics.

Thirdly, *no*, our monastery would not include nuns. Particularly not "for breeding purposes." Perhaps we should send you a pamphlet on our order.

Fourthly, *no*, it would not be possible to make you a "Vice-

Abbot" of our proposed monastery. In the first place, we would have only a Prior at our head, and not an Abbot. In the second place, leadership positions (or "Fuhrer posts" as you put it) can only be held by those taking orders in the brotherhood. Again, perhaps a pamphlet might be in order.

Finally, we must stress that in the event that we accept your funding we would be in no way beholden to you or your organization. We must in all ways remain independent irrespective of our needs. As our motto says: "The Cross is steady while the world turns." We are certain you understand this.

Let us not end on a sour note though! We are most grateful for your kind offer of support and look forward to creating, with your help, a hermitage worthy of our humble order.

Sincerely,

Brother Rodriguez, Prior Prospective, Grand Hermitage of the Argentine Highlands (Proposed). January 15, 1873.

From: Prior (Pending) Alphonse Rodriquez, Nido de Aquila, Argentina, July 22, 1878.

To: Bernard Forster, Superior Leader, German People's League (Original).

Dear Herr Forster,

Greetings from the Argentine! I am happy to confirm that the brothers have agreed to name our abbey (really a priory) as you suggested. We are now The Abbey of the Eagles! Kloster Adler! This took some doing as we Carthusians do not normally name our monasteries after animals. Particularly birds of prey. Still, a small concession for so great a contribution.

You will be happy to know that building proceeds apace. No small feat given that we can only speak with contractors once a month. As you know, we did have a few concerns about the architectural plans you originally sent. So much stone! And to be lifted so high! We were further confused by your tendency to call the monastery walls "battlements" and the church walls "ramparts." With whom would we battle? Everyone is so nice here. But we quickly put all this, as well as your habit of referring to the Abbey (really the Priory) as a "last redoubt for the German People," down to harmless idiosyncrasy. And the buildings look very impressive. Especially, if I may say so, the scriptorium. Again, a most unnecessary addition given current publishing technology and our Carthusian vows of isolation, but nevertheless beautiful to look at. Very "traditional values" indeed.

On a rather more serious matter. We, too, are very concerned about the local Jews living near the monastery. We have set our lay brothers about the task of converting them (not an ordinary mission for Carthusians, but extraordinary times call for extraordinary actions). These conversions are going, I must admit, rather slowly. I realize that this was not the solution to the local Jewish problem that you suggested, but we think it best. The days of what you call "warrior monks" are, I am actually relieved to say, long past.

I will also need to disappoint you, regretfully, on the matter of allowing you and other "colonists" and "People's Founders" to stay at our abbey (really priory) as guests. Our Carthusian vows forbid such contact with secular persons. Other orders allow it, ours does not. Perhaps the pamphlets we sent you did not adequately stress this point. We certainly cannot become a "monastic hostel for the German People." You are, of course, welcome in the town (you are building it after all), but you cannot come to the monastery. Given how much we have conceded to you on the matter of "property rights" in our monastery, I'm sure you can concede this point to us.

But let us not end on a sour note! Soon we will inaugurate the Abbey of the Eagles! (Really Priory.) The brothers and I intend to mark the occasion with a moment of silence. We wish, naturally enough, that you and our funders could be here for this, but, alas, the Carthusian Statutes will not allow it. We will send you photos. Reminded always of our motto: "The Cross is steady while the world turns."

All our best,

Prior Rodriguez, Abbey (Priory) of the Eagles. July 22, 1878.

From: Prior Superior, Alphonse Rodriguez, Kloster Adler, December 5, 1882.

To: Bernard Forster, Ultimate Autocrat, German People's League (Singular).

Dear Herr Forster,

I write to you now to again thank you for your recent visit to the Abbey of the Eagles. It was so lovely to meet you at last! We don't normally take meals in the church (or even together for that matter) but the church is, as you put it, "the safest place in the monastery should the Jews attack." We were also most gratified at your obvious delight in our making you honorary vice-Abbot of the Kloster Adler. You may of course keep the Robes of Installation, but the brothers have asked if you might return the twelfth-century bible you borrowed. A mere over-sight I'm sure.

The brothers and I were most intrigued by your suggestion that the Abbey needed "easier access." Yes the stairs through the mountain are most arduous. I appreciate that you had "breathing difficulties" on your way up. But I remind you that we are a severely cloistered order. We never leave.

Finally, I was troubled to hear that you found the town, or "colony," less than ideal. Altitude sickness can be distressing. The Jews *are* somewhat "too close for comfort." And again, the stairs. Perhaps you are correct that the jungles of Paraguay would be more appropriate as a location for the "New Germany." The brothers and I wish you all the luck in the world there.

Sincerely,

(Vice) Abbot Rodriguez, Kloster Adler. December 5, 1882.

From: Prior Superior, Martin Klaus, Kloster Adler, September 17, 1889.
To: Elizabeth Forster-Nietzsche, German People's League (Defunct)
Dear Frau Forster-Nietzsche,

We are most grieved to hear of the recent suicide of your husband, so long our benefactor. Paraguay can be a hard country. I write to assure you, as you resolve his estate, that we at the Abbey both honor his name and comply with the requirements of the Writ of Ownership as per previous correspondence. As you settle his affairs I ask that you consider making a gift of the monastery to the Carthusian Brothers, as I am certain your husband would have wanted.

If this proves somehow unacceptable, we at least need to know to whom this writ will be transferred. Who might be our new and generous benefactor? We have every confidence that you will direct any legacy falling into your hands with utmost concern for the principles which underlie it.

With condolences,
Prior Klaus, Kloster Adler. September 17, 1889.

A hotel room in Salzburg – day

The room of Trevor and Kip. Kip looks his normal self. No wig, goatee, or late sixties psychedelic hipster finery. Just his own, unadorned, youthful innocent face. He fusses with an elaborate makeup kit while reading a paper. Trevor uses a small mirror to fine-tune his moustache. His shaving and trimming kit looks only a bit less elaborate than Kip's Lon Chaney prep-box. On the table beside the mirror, a scattering of documents lie ready for inspection, the takings of last night's adventure.

Kip, "I think I figured out the message."

Irritation crosses Trevor's face, but he re-contorts his expression to the task of mustache trimming, "I'm quite sure

I don't care."

Kip reads from the paper, "Beware Gay Astronaut. Halftrain."

Trevor, "I recall the message and its provenance."

Kip pauses a moment, "I don't think it should have said *Gay Astronaut*. I think he meant to say, *Beware Gas Tranquilizer: Knockout.*"

Trevor puts away his kit, "Yes, I am aware that while we were on the alert for a joyous, but dangerous space traveler, we were in fact all the while imperiled by tranquilizer gas emitted from the safe. I don't recall a great deal of last night after I opened the wretched thing, but I do seem to hazily recollect that it contained no gay astronauts."

Silence.

Kip, "I'm just saying. We get these warnings for a reason. We should try to figure them out."

Trevor puts down his razor and takes up the papers beside him, "While you have engaged in the untimely decryption of the mad ravings of the idiot Halftrain, I have made useful discoveries in the cache of documents we recovered last night from their gaseous repository. Discoveries that I have every reason to believe will launch—if you will excuse the expression—our moribund investigation into new and productive territory."

Kip brightens. He loves it when Trevor gets on a roll, "They mention Formula XOX?"

Trevor takes on a sarcastic expression, "Why yes. They even mention us by name. *Here Kip and Trevor you shall find Formula XOX and discover all of its esoteric subtleties—read on stalwart fellows.* Mystery finally solved."

Kip shows patience with such outbursts, "What then?"

Now Trevor lays it out. He spreads documents before Kip, "Look here. If we presume that von Richter received the topmost document most lately, and thus from the courier in the fedora whom we have so oft noted in our investigations, then," he points to the paper, "note from whence it comes."

He presents the paper to Kip holding his finger on the relevant line.

Kip reads it, "Odessa Laboratories, Dusseldorf."

Nodding, Trevor continues, "And that envelope contains an account of blood samples obtained in said laboratory and a description of its *distillation*. Whatever that might mean." Undaunted by new mysteries, Trevor presses forward, "Further, the document mentions a Doctor Damarung, which name has so often been invoked in documents pertaining to our investigation."

Kip, "The sinister Doctor Damarung raises his head once again!"

Trevor, "Yes, well, strictly speaking none have called him *sinister*, though we might infer such from his clear interest in blood and presumed interest in secret formulae. But if I might return to my point."

Kip, "Sorry."

Trevor, "Attending again to our bounty from last night, and having covered now the topmost documents, consider that when we look back further in the cache of documents," Trevor again handles the documents, "we find a regular correspondence between von Richter and this laboratory. The aforementioned *Odessa Laboratories*."

Kip, "All important enough to keep secret in a wall safe!"

Trevor looks pleased with himself.

Kip, "So what's next?"

Trevor, "Well if I were in search of a secret formula—and I very much am—I would be on my way to Dusseldorf."

Kip smiles. He turns to a what looks like a typewriter crossed with an octopus mating with a miniature ham radio set. With such a device, and two strong arms to carry it, one can contact Interpol, fully encrypted. "I'll notify headquarters on the Lector."

Trevor smiles.

Kip, "They may have some intelligence for us about dangers in Dusseldorf."

Trevor frowns.

Outside the Goldberg farm – Argentina

A small farm, much like the Cohen farm, with a central opening before the farmhouse, vineyards to one side, coop and barn to another, and hedgerows giving the place a further sense of demarcation and enclosure. Marcy stands with Papa Cohen while talking with Mr. Goldberg.

Chris walks apart from them with Katrina in tow. Before him lies a little graveyard, fenced in and containing a scattering of tombstones all commemorated with a Star of David. He walks past this to two rather fresher mounds, clearly outside of, and at a distance from, the Goldberg family graveyard.

As Chris makes his way there, Marcy questions a clearly reluctant Mr. Goldberg. She asks him, "So sheep killed too? How many?"

Mr. Goldberg, "Oh, some. Not so many." Mr. Goldberg looks nervously at Papa Cohen. Papa Cohen gives a slight nod and Goldberg, a bit reassured, goes on, "Maybe twenty."

Marcy, "Twenty! In how many days?"

Mr. Goldberg, "Maybe three days. The past three days."

Marcy, "And they all died by wounds?"

Papa Cohen nods for him to continue.

Mr. Goldberg, "Yes. Deep cuts. Chewed up. Not eaten, just chewed up."

Apart from them Chris leans over the mound of a fresh grave, human sized, not sheep sized. The dirt has not yet had time to sink. Katrina pokes at the dirt with a stick.

Chris, "Not here baby."

Katrina, "Bad dirt."

Chris looks over his shoulder to see Hadassah not far away, watching him. In the distance, Chris can just barely hear Marcy's conversation.

Marcy, "Do wolves live near the mountains?"

Mr. Goldberg, "No wolves!"

Papa Cohen, "We have no wolves in Argentina. Our closest animal, they call a wolf, but it looks more like a fox. It does not live near the mountains."

Chris has moved on to a hedgerow. Stuck in the leaves of the hedge he sees a tuft of dark hair. Or fur. Or really some fibrous in-between material both fur and hair, but not quite either. Chris inspects it carefully. He bends down to Katrina, "Bring me all of this you can find." She heads off happy to have a mission. As Chris stands up he finds Hadassah practically at his shoulder. Chris slightly jumps back as he sees her. They look eye to eye for a moment. Then she walks away.

Watching her go, Chris looks past her at the mountain view, almost Alpine in its beauty. On a low mountain not far as the crow flies, he sees a structure, several really, enclosed by a wall. Chris recognizes the architecture, and its historical misplacement on a low Andean ridge.

The buildings look like a monastery.

Across the yard, Chris can hear Marcy continue her increasingly unproductive questioning of Mr. Goldberg. Chris walks over.

Marcy, "Have there been any circuses in the village lately?" This puzzles both Goldberg and Cohen. Marcy tries what she takes to be a clarification, "I'm thinking like with performing bears." Still confusing. "That might have escaped?" Goldberg shakes his head. No. No escaped bears.

Chris approaches as Marcy nods her thanks, "Thank you Mr. Goldberg. Rest assured, Interpol will get to the bottom of this." Mr. Goldberg walks with Papa Cohen back to the farmhouse, leaving Chris with Marcy.

Chris, "Interpol works the case."

Her defense, "These people are suffering. Attacks in the night. Dead sheep. Slaughtered."

Chris, "And alpacas."

Marcy, "Alpacas."

Chris, "And Marcy Gainer will solve their mystery. On her

husband's working vacation."

Marcy's shoulders slump, "She would if even a single clue had been left."

Katrina runs up, her arms fully laden with great wads of dark hair-fur. Katrina stops before her dad and to him says: "I found lots!" Chris pats her head and looks at Marcy. Marcy looks puzzled.

In a car – on the street – Washington, D.C. day

Natasha drives while Rafe sits beside her studying a single piece of paper.

Rafe, "So she's *out to sea*. That seems vital. On a ship? Lost at sea? Why wouldn't Interpol just call the Coast Guard?" Rafe ponders this logical pickle, "She's on a submarine maybe."

Natasha shows no interest.

Rafe continues his meditation, "The fourth richest man in the world, and he's in Palacia? Or is he the fourth richest man in Palacia, and we don't know his current location? But probably Palacia." Rafe pauses to ponder, "Where is Palacia? Out to sea. An island maybe?" A longer pause now, "Dookies?"

Rafe looks bollixed again. Another mystery: "Over-blown penile restitution." A bit more of a think, "This Doctor Damarung has far less skill at the restoration of penises than people have made out." Pausing to think does not seem to be helping, "So he's kidnaped Marcy ... and has her on a submarine ... and must be stopped at the coast before he," Rafe strains to find the answer, "gives her to nasty desiccated asthmatics. Damn. I almost had it."

Natasha points to the paper, "A toy for children."

Rafe studies on, "Do you know an Agent Nina? Because I think she has Marcy."

Natasha, "You are boy with secret decoder ring from Captain Cosmo cereal box."

Rafe, "I happened to have *loved* Captain Cosmo, and it took *ten* box tops to get the decoder ring. And if I had the thing still we wouldn't be half so far behind." He studies the page. "The opera uses the old cape routine." He thinks. "Not a new one. The old one. The standard one from the old days. The good old days of the one cape routine. And performed as part of the aria. The extra aria. The song you never expected." Oh, for a decoder ring. "With the Diva doing the—old—cape routine. Like a bull-fighting opera. Did anyone fight a bull in *Carmen*?"

Natasha again points to the paper, "Into this black hole all reason and sense will forever be sucked, never to escape."

Rafe, "Fine. How do you propose we find Marcy? Where are you driving us?"

Natasha, "To home of Marcy."

Okay. Admittedly not a terrible place to start. Rafe examines the paper, "An opera ... performed at sea ... for people with a dry cough." Nope.

Outside the Odessa laboratory – Dusseldorf

Nighttime. A modest lab building of no particular note, a sign that says, *Odessa Laboratories*, a parking lot, empty of all but a single car, a street before the parking lot, a dim yellow streetlight on the street, and finally, below this, Kip and Trevor, stand.

They wear overcoats against the winter cold and have stocking caps on their heads, bundled up and ready to be pulled down to conceal their faces. Why this should be necessary for Kip remains unclear since he has outfitted himself in a full beard.

Trevor, "I cannot fathom your attachment to these ridiculous disguises. Who here might recognize you?"

Kip, "You wouldn't understand. It's art."

Trevor, "It's lunacy."

Knowing it will annoy Trevor, "I decoded a warning from Halftrain about this operation."

Trevor, "I have no interest in further absurd warnings

from headquarters. Now if Marcy were still our contact, it would be different. But Halftrain."

Silence.

Kip, "They seemed to think it important." He waits. "Double Urgent message the Lector said."

Trevor sighs in defeat. Kip takes a piece of paper from his pocket and reads in the light of the streetlamp. "Beware Pretense of Expensive Substitutes." A moment of silence in honor of the profundity.

Trevor, "Substitutes for what? And how can their mere pretense, whatever the expense, threaten us in the least? Pointless drivel."

Within the gaze of Trevor, a figure emerges from the lab door. It wears a black overcoat and, rather improbably given the weather, a gray fedora.

Trevor, "But look here if you want to see something really interesting." The man in the fedora enters a car and drives off, momentarily splashing the beam from his headlights on Kip and Trevor as they turn away, hands in pockets, as if fending off the cold.

Kip, "He's just made a drop."

Trevor, "And I'll warrant put it straight into the safe as we see no one here to take it."

Kip, "Then let's get to it. Get out of the cold at least."

Trevor, "Yes. Time to warm up."

Inside the Odessa Laboratory, Kip and Trevor creep through the hallways, masks down, flashlights their only illumination.

Kip, "Do you know where to find it?"

Trevor, "I found the plans in the local architectural office. They built the safe into a wall in an office just past a large storage room." They walk on towards a door ahead, illuminated in the beams of their flashlights. "Just ahead."

Kip, "I can't see a thing in this mask."

Trevor, "Then take it off."

Kip, "I can't, it's stuck on the beard."

Trevor turns in frustration. He stuffs his flashlight into the shoulder strap of his overcoat to free his hands while Kip holds his beam on the mask and the entangling beard. Trevor's beam shines on the wall behind them. Trevor struggles to work Kip's mask around the beard.

Trevor, "If you must concoct these absurd concealments might you at least use less glue for their attachment?" As Trevor struggles with the mask, focused only on that, the beam of his flashlight illuminates a sign on the wall. It says: WARNUNG EXPLOSIV SUBSTANZEN.

Kip, "I've got it now."

Trevor retrieves his flashlight and heads toward the office door at the end of the hall. He picks its lock with the skilled hand and hardy nerve of the expert tumbler he is and opens the door. Kip follows.

Inside the office, Trevor prepares the large safe with plastic explosive and a long line of wire to a detonator. "Tip over the desk, I'll use it for further protection."

Kip tips over a desk, leaving its underside facing a long window and the desktop facing the safe on the opposite wall. Kip asks, "Why not tumble it? You're going to hurt someone with C4."

Trevor, "Fine cracksman I'd be if I didn't know my way around explosive charges. I'll not give them another chance to gas me. Besides, the way I've arranged the explosives all of the blast will go into the storage area behind the safe." Trevor completes the wiring and reels out the line to the overturned desk. Trevor says, "You wait outside the window, and I'll set off the blast, clear the safe, and off we go to the car. Crack teamwork."

Kip nods. He hops out the window into the dark and cold night. He walks a bit away, breathing the fresh air. He looks to the sky; the beautiful Milky Way. Stars painted across the heavens. The cosmos turning in celestial silence. A thick layer of snow on the ground reflects the moon's rays. Kip sees his breath before him. He marvels at the dampened quite of a snow-covered night. A clear, crisp evening hushed in nature's wonder.

Then a great hellish explosion goes off behind him. Trevor flies past Kip to the ground, accompanied by an enormous flutter of papers. For a moment Kip can't quite process. How did Trevor gain the power of flight? Why does Trevor-in-flight spew great swaths of paper in his wake? Then Kip gets it. He runs to Trevor. He lifts him to a sitting position.

Kip, "Trevor! Trevor!"

Trevor comes round; scorched and dazed. Trevor looks Kip blankly in the eyes, Trevor says, "Mother?"

Kip, "Thank god." Kip lets go of Trevor who falls back. Kip leaps up snatching papers from the air. Kip does this while Trevor staggers to his feet. Kip shouts, "Grab papers! Grab papers!"

Trevor rights himself, eyes unfocused. A paper lands, wind-pressed upon his face. He pulls it off, looks at it—nope, no comprehension—he drops it.

Kip tucks his scorched, smoking documents under his arm and grabs Trevor, directing him away from the scene. "Come on!" He guides Trevor away, "Great explosion by the way, a real jolt."

Letters – 1991-2003

From: Dr. Hans Gertz, Research Director, Biomax Laboratories, Dusseldorf DE, June 3, 1991.

To: Frederick "Count" Orlok, General Manager, Odessa Operations, Nido de Aquila, AG.

Dear Mr. Orlok,

Our Chief Financial Officer has just informed me of your interest in our research here at Biomax Labs. He asked me to give you a brief summary. I here happily comply.

Principally, we conduct experiments on animal subjects (humanely treated according to the research bylaws of the *United Nations Summary International Accord for Research Activity on Live Animals (Appendix Eight)* and the *Federal*

Republic of Germany Rules and Regulations Governing Animal Research (inclusive of Recommended Practices Subsections 1-27). Our research concerns the manipulation of genotype information and replication structures at the genetic level (acting always in accord with rules adapted by the General Conference of the United Nations Educational, Scientific, and Cultural Organization Covering Genetic Research as embodied by the United Nations General Assembly Resolution on Genetic Testing in Human and Animal Subjects Under Humane Conditions, as well as those enforced and recommended by the Committee on Safety for Genetic Experimentation on/with Research Animals and Live Research Subjects of the Ministry of Public Safety for the Federal Republic of Germany).

Our overarching research aim is to apply animal genes to helping humans overcome illness and disease (while being fully committed to the aims, goals, and rules set out in the Professional Association of Genetic and Biomedical Researchers of Europe: Ethical and Best Practices Guidelines, and while maintaining strict records as dictated by the Associated Researchers for Ethical Treatment of Animal Genes: Records and Archives Protocols—Amended Section VII).

Also we do not use pets.

I hope that this brief summary of our activity, and our assurance of ethical and responsible research practice under the rule of law and democratically recommended moral guidelines for humane treatment of all persons and sentient beings, gives you some idea of Biomax Laboratories research effort. Of course I understand that you may have some further questions so please write to me at any time.

Sincerely,

Dr. Hans Gertz, Research Director, Biomax Laboratories.
June 3, 1991.

From: Dr. Hans Gertz, Research Director, Odessa/Biomax Laboratories, Dusseldorf DE, September 1, 1993.
To: Count Frederick Orlok, Director, Odessa Industries,

Nido de Aquila, AG.

Dear Count Orlok,

Our CFO has just informed me of your considerable investment in Odessa/Biomax Laboratories. Welcome on board! I write in response to your letter of January 8th of last year (please accept my apologies for this delayed response as well as for any misunderstandings regarding your honorifics). I will try here to answer your questions and respond to your many interesting and helpful suggestions.

While it is true that we "crack the very code of life" as you so charmingly put it, we do not do so in order to "create the superior man," but rather for the benefit of all mankind (or rather person-kind, according to latest convention). An understandable misunderstanding.

While it is true that we seek to help people overcome illness and disease, it is not the case that "inferior blood" constitutes an illness. Nor is "decadent genome" a scientific term. Admittedly, contemporary scientific nomenclature can be confusing.

While it is true that we seek to "enhance life," we have not actually investigated the "search for personal immortality." But what an intriguing suggestion! Although some of us were a bit confused, and others more than a bit concerned, at your following phrase: "for those of the higher types." I have assured my staff that you would have us discover personal immortality for all types (or possibly that you meant to deny types for humans, we currently research the *Annals of Ethical Research Practice: Linguistic Standards and Guidelines* for the correct understanding of your phrase).

While it is true that our DNA research seeks alterations in the entirety of an individual subject's genes through the "injection of strong animal DNA" (quibbling a bit over "strong"), our research has not advanced to the point of "creating eternal vigor." And yes, crocodiles do live a surprisingly long time, but, alas, we have no ability at this time to leverage crocodile longevity through DNA injection into humans. Frankly, we organize our research around applications in the field of congenital disease and cancer.

We do not engage in "cloning."

I hope this clears matters up somewhat. We at Odessa/Biomax Laboratories prize clear communications about aims and practices between our scientists and our investors. I have no doubt that apart from the odd miscommunication we are all pulling on the same team in pursuit of the same goal.

Finally, let me add that of course we would be happy to offer a position to the man you describe as an "exemplary researcher" who has been "unjustly maligned for his revolutionary ideas." We here at Odessa/Biomax are great opponents of injustice and pride ourselves on being open-minded. And considering your generous offer to fully subsidize your candidate's research here, we can overlook any less than satisfactory recommendations from "benighted institutions of higher learning." So by all means send Dr. Damarung here to be the *Count Orlok Researcher into Longevity*. We look forward to meeting him.

Most sincerely,

Dr. Hans Gertz, Research Director, Odessa/Biomax Laboratories. September 1, 1993.

From: Dr. Hans Gertz, Research Administer, Odessa Laboratories, Dusseldorf, DE, May 23, 1998.
To: Count Frederick von Orlok, President, Odessa Industries, Nido de Aquila, AG.

Dear General Count von Orlok,

I write to you once again to express concern over your "prodigy" Dr. Damarung. I must again preface my remarks with the assurance that we here at Odessa Laboratories have approached "the good Doctor" with very open minds (as you urged us to). We batted not an eye when we found that he received his PhD from the *Seat of Eagles University of the Andes*. We batted the odd eye upon discovering that he received his medical degree from the *New German Reich School of Experimental Medicine* in Paraguay. We recently discovered he did his dissertation on "Human/Animal Hybridism; Prospects and Potential," and this led to eyes, frankly, flung wide open. Further searches of the professional literature (and to be honest, considerable searches beyond this) have revealed a pattern of papers keyed to such phrases as "racial strengthening," "Aryanization," and "degenerate genomes." These do not represent best research practices in our opinion. I know you weary of references to the current professional literature on research ethics, but there must be some way to get across the seriousness of this issue. I struggle for the right way to put the matter.

It is never acceptable to publish the reference: "Mengele, J., 1943."

And the opinions he expresses here at the lab (confining ourselves just to his "scientific" opinions in the interest of brevity) indicate a fundamental lack of soundness. We here can hardly comprehend his meaning when he speaks of the "inherent scientific wisdom of the volk." We suspect something of his meaning when he speaks favorably of the "mystical bond of Aryan science and nature." And we are disturbingly confident of his meaning when he asks: "does this ethical ban include Jews?"

I appreciate that you have written to Dr. Damarung about his "mis-comportment" after my earlier letters. We all appreciate that. I worry, though, that matters have gone beyond mere office behavior. When a scientist leans over a microscope while remarking on the distinction between second and third stage "were-beastism," I think matters have gone rather far past infelicitous expression. And what should we make of his request for safe storage of "viral lycanthropy" specimens? In compliance with your frequent requests, I restrain myself from citing the relevant professional standards but merely reiterate the general point that we are a level five biohazard genetic lab, and that entails certain dangers and attendant responsibilities.

I am quite certain that none of Dr. Damarung's experiments meet with your approval. I realize he has reported to you certain "favorable results," but these could be of no account to a responsible businessman such as yourself. We have bent over backwards on the matter of Dr. Damarung, but I think we have at last reached the point where you must draw a line.

Ever confident in your judgement,

Dr. Hans Gertz, Research Administer, Odessa Laboratories. May 23, 1998.

From: Victor von Richter, Director General, Odessa Laboratories, Dusseldorf DE, July 9, 2003.

To: Dr. General Count von Orlok, Supreme Head, ODESSA, Kehlsteinhausdorf, AG.

Dear Leader,

I am happy to report that all aspects of Odessa Industries' laboratory and scientific work have been "regularized." All personnel have been vetted or eliminated. All records have been secured. All correspondence now proceeds by courier. The last of the good Doctor's samples and equipment have been sent to his facility at the Place of the Sacred Relic.

All Glory to the Final Resolution!

Sincerely,

Director von Richter. July 9, 2003.

Within Marcy's apartment – midday

A modest apartment, lots of anthropology books scattered about, toys neatly placed in a toy chest except for the odd rattle on the floor. A large wooden doll house of classic design rests against the wall. Neat and tidy, no signs of struggle. A shame that, since signs of struggle would be of help at least. Natasha and Rafe have completed anything that might constitute a search for clues. The only signs of illegal entry they have found are the ones they made, and the only clue to the disappearance of Marcy they have discovered is the simultaneous absence of her family.

Rafe speculates, "Maybe her husband Chris has some sort of erectile disfunction issue."

At the doorway to the apartment a woman appears. Janet Ellison, a youngish woman who by no stretch of the imagination could be mistaken for an international woman of mystery and fulltime femme fatale. She looks like anyone's neighbor might. And for the very good reason that she is, indeed, someone's neighbor.

Janet Ellison, ever helpful, asks, "Hello? Can I help you?"

Rafe instantly deploys his Master of Distraction skills, "No worries ma'am, we're with pest control, just here about the rats. Securing the rats right now."

Janet, honestly alarmed, "Rats!?!"

Rafe, "No worries ma'am, caught all the rats—put them in the car—van—our van—the pest van. We just came back up to tag the droppings. Done in just a minute."

Janet, "I know you're not pest control."

Rafe, "You're right of course. My partner and I are here on a mattress inspection. Mrs. Gainer wanted to return it, but of course we need to inspect it first. For soiling—not to be indelicate. Mrs. Gainer's in the other room."

Janet, "Marcy isn't here."

Rafe, "No, we thought it would be best if she didn't stay for the inspection; she is awfully attached to that mattress."

Natasha looks just mildly amused by all this.

Janet, "I know you. You're Rafe Riley, you work with Marcy." Rafe looks taken aback. Janet nods to Natasha, "Hello Natasha."

Natasha nods to Janet, "Janet."

The light bulb goes off for Rafe, "Janet. Janet Ellison, the party. You live next door." Good to have that settled.

Natasha, "Janet, we cannot find Marcy. She goes missing."

Janet, "Missing?"

Rafe, "We're looking for Marcy. We aren't really concerned with the mattress at all."

Janet had inferred this already, "Marcy left the country. She went with Chris and Katrina. I don't know their final destination. Some field project she had set up for Chris. She did say they would pass through Buenos Aires."

Rafe snaps his fingers, "Buenos Aires! Not Bonus Arias! They are doing the old cape dance in Buenos Aires! This is all falling into place!"

Natasha looks doubtful. She asks Janet: "Where does husband Chris Gainer make study."

Rafe shrugs, sensible enough line of inquiry, given the lack of a decoder ring.

Within a Dusseldorf hotel room – morning

The Dusseldorf Grand Hotel offers firm beds, downy double duvets and a minibar with a tracking and charging system that took Kip most of ten minutes to disable. A bit modern for a proper German vacation experience, but fine for spies on the dodge. Trevor uses a battery powered precision electric razor to trim off the singed ends of his moustache. Kip ponders a message.

Kip, "Pretty close if you think about it."

Trevor does not want to think about it.

Kip, "Damn close I'd say."

Trevor stops his shave to attend to Kip, "Sorry old man, can't hear you, what with the constant ringing in my ears."

Kip reads, "*Beware Pretense of Expensive Substitutes*. That must have meant *Beware Presence of Explosive Substances*."

Trevor taps his ear, "Ring-ring old man. Nothing getting through."

Kip, "Very close really." Kip considers his thesis, "Compared to the others."

Trevor packs away his shaver, "Through the clanging bells I *have* managed to find a few apposite papers from those you snatched from the smoky air surrounding what remained of the Odessa Laboratories." Trevor pulls documents from a pile on the bed to show Kip; some only half-documents, owing to having been partly turned to ash. "You see here on this document—the part not burned away—that it's a report on something it describes as a potentially dangerous *viral extract*. I would say, parenthetically, that the lot we have made central to our inquires would be the last people on earth humanity should entrust with extracting viruses. Their careless signage of laboratory hazards and general disregard for occupational health and safety alone should disqualify them from any form of scientific extraction. But I digress."

Kip, "You have every right to digress."

Trevor offers another bit of evidence, "See this page here, evidently the sole survivor of a longer missive, it makes a request for further…" he shudders, "*secretions*, to be purified into a *viral extract*. Thankful as I am to be spared the details of this part of their endeavor—"

Kip, "Sinister endeavor."

Trevor, "Sinister endeavor—nonetheless, I cannot but notice that they, the writers of these reports, appear oddly circumspect about provenance and procedure. Especially odd considering the supposed scientific nature of their activities. It cannot help but cast a certain pall over the entire operation. Giving their un-named research an aspect of the … uh…"

Kip, "Sinister."

Trevor, "Menacing. In any event," Trevor displays a last document, "have a look, finally, at this, the *piece de resistance*. It looks to be an invoice, recording the receipt of a consignment of … fluids … for purification. A process not otherwise elaborated on, but bearing, mind you, a parenthetical note: *XO*."

Kip studies the texts before him, "Well I grant the relevance, but where does it lead?"

Trevor, "Frightfully good question if I hear you correctly,

though barely even odds of that anymore I'm afraid. In answer to your question, I point out that all of these documents have been addressed either to, or from, or signed by someone at, the *Brothers of Mercy Asylum of Budapest.* An institution apparently in the charge of one Doctor Hoffbrau." Trevor notices something for the first time, "Odd that the correspondents all write in English, considering the general Teutonic flavor of all the names. But don't piddle on your own luck, I say."

Kip, "So that means?" Kip loves to hear Trevor draw a conclusion.

Trevor, "Well, if I were on the trail of a villain wearing a gray fedora, and I do believe I am, I would now be on my way to: Budapest."

Kip nods, "I'll notify headquarters."

Trevor fails to suppress a grimace.

Outside at the Levy farm – Argentina

We see the remains of a shed. The roof and three sides still stand, barely, but the front wall has been completely crushed. The detritus of the shed's contents lie on its dirt floor. Based on the visible fragments, something has reduced this pottery shed to a collection of pot fragments.

Marcy stands with Mr. Levy, looking at the shed. Chris stands apart from them watching as Katrina hops around the scene playing. Well behind them all stands Papa Cohen.

Marcy, "Could the wind have done this?"

Levy looks skeptical, "We have wind. Mostly the sheds survive it."

Marcy, "Maybe vandals? You know, teenagers on a lark?"

Chris shakes his head in disbelief.

Mr. Levy, "We're a long way from anyone else. Mostly no one drives by. Just the Cohens, the Goldbergs. People we know."

Marcy, "Could you show me the alpaca pen?"

Mr. Levy, "Not much left to see, but come with me."

Marcy and Mr. Levy walk away from the shed, leaving Chris and Katrina. Chris walks into the ruined shed. He bends down to inspect the ground. Perhaps rain blew in onto the dirt floor on the night of the attack. Although dried and hardened now, Chris can see a distinct print upon the ground. But a print of what? Too large for a dog; to broad for a man. The print reveals the maker had an instep, but maybe, what? Claws on the feet? Katrina hops in and looks with Daddy.

Katrina, "Paw."

Chris, "Big paw."

Katrina puts her foot into the print, it is bigger than her foot by far. Chris hoists her up. He exits the shed. Looking in the distance he sees the mountain monastery again. The change in angle more clearly shows its bell-tower, visible above the monastery walls, but the angle does nothing to erase the impression of historical misplacement.

Closer at hand, Chris sees Hadassah guiding Mama Levy towards him. Mama Levy trusts Hadassah, but strangers, maybe not so much. They stop and Hadassah motions Mama Levy forward while she, Hadassah, stays at a distance. Mama Levy hesitates as she comes nearer, but she smiles at Katrina. Mama Levy hasn't had a child that young in many years.

Chris smiles at her, "Do you speak English?"

Mama Levy nods and continues to look longingly at Katrina, "I am Avigail Levy."

Chris, "I'm Chris Gainer. This is Katrina."

Katrina, "I talk too much."

Mama Levy laughs. Chris feels very much like people watch him. He sees Hadassah off in front of him. Glancing left Chris notes that Ehud stands not far off, watching as well.

Chris nods toward the shed, "Quite a mess something made."

Mama Levy stiffens.

Katrina, "Uh oh."

Mama Levy smiles just a little.

Chris, "Would you like to hold Katrina? She loves strangers." Katrina holds out her arms in *take-me* position. Mama Levy smiles broadly and takes her.

Away from this, with Mr. Levy beside her, Marcy inspects the alpaca pen, such as remains of it. For something has reduced it to kindling wood. Marcy can see the alpaca carcasses scattered about, "So a total loss."

Mr. Levy, "A few ran off, my boys chase after them, but the rest." He gestures at the scene before them. Marcy views an alpaca apocalypse. Fresh bodies cover the ground, wooden fencing lies about smashed to splinters. Something clearly passed through here with a great deal of violence and an intense dislike of alpacas.

Marcy, "Did anything leave tracks?"

Mr. Levy, "I don't know from tracks."

Marcy looks around. She sees Ehud and Hadassah watching Chris intently, keeping their distance. Beyond them, she sees Chris listening to an older woman talking to him fulsomely as the woman tickles Katrina.

Marcy, "If you had to rate from one to ten, ten being most unusual, one being ho hum every day, how would you rate this?"

Mr. Levy, "You mean both the ripped apart shed and the destruction of the fences and the slaughter of alpacas? Or do you want I should rate each one separately?"

Marcy, "Altogether. A comprehensive ranking, weighted anyway you like."

Mr. Levy, "Well. That would take some math."

Marcy wonders what Interpol interrogation technique she needs to deploy to get information out of these people. She glances over to watch Chris again.

Chris listens, Mama Levy speaks, "It would happen. Always sometimes, never not at all, but lately, this last two weeks…" She shrugs.

Chris, "As bad as five years ago?"

Mama Levy nods. She bounces Katrina up and down. She sees Marcy approaching.

Chris, "And you don't feel you can say anything," he looks for the word, "*descriptive*, about it?"

Mama Levy shakes her head. Marcy arrives behind Chris.

Mama Levy whispers to Chris, "The authorities. They do not like us. They would not understand certain ... necessities."

Chris, "Right. One more thing. Do you think, possibly, someone in the valley may have had a seventh son?"

Mama nods, most definitely, "Yes." She hands Katrina back to Chris, smiles politely at Marcy, and heads back toward her house.

Marcy, "I'm starting to wonder which of us is working on this vacation."

Chris, "Welcome to my world."

Katrina, "No fighting." She wags her fingers.

Within the Abbey library – day

A needle withdraws from an arm. And once again, Doctor Damarung stands at the giving end, and Count Orlok at the receiving.

Count Orlok, "Most refreshing Herr Doctor."

Orlok stands, roles down his sleeve and puts on his coat. The coat looks more than a little like a German general staff officer's coat from the Second World War, right down to badges and medals, though historians and uniform buffs would be hard pressed to corollate any of the uniform's insignia with actual Wehrmacht ranks, units, or decorations. The uniform bears the marks of creativity, and also tailor's marks. It apparently needs to be let out a bit since its last wearing.

Orlok gives a casual wave of his hand, and his tailor steps in to complete the measurements. The tailor wears a brown uniform that would itself have been quite at home in Weimar Germany. Not a friendly, relaxed, apolitical home, but some of the homes. One might refer to the uniform as *vintage brown-shirt*. This appears to be the staff uniform of the Abbey of the Eagles, though at the moment the brown-shirt ensemble lacks a memorable arm band from Ye Olde Days.

And of the library itself, we find it in transition; a conversion to match its owner's wardrobe. Several men in brown-shirts carefully lower the great portrait of Mademoiselle Guimard. Another removes a bust of Voltaire, while still another removes a rococo French coffee pot. All around Orlok, brown-shirted men remove the precious artifacts of cultured life. Other objects, still covered with canvass and wrapped in twine, await placement and unwrapping. Orlok disregards the welter and makes points to his tailor as two men wait on him. Before Orlok, and opposite each other, thus forming a sinister triangle, stand Doctor Damarung and Karl.

Count Orlok, "Your report Karl."

Karl, "You already know of Otto von Bruzing's," Karl hesitates, "fate." Orlok waves Karl on, a single benediction more than suffices for Otto. Karl continues, "I fear I can report no success. The Juden will not move. They have not sense enough to be frightened. Such cowardice. They do not contact the authorities for help, but," Karl can hardly find the words to express his outrage, "bury their problems."

Doctor Damarung offers a suggestion, "Your excellency. Give me the task. I can unleash upon them such ferocity."

Count Orlok, "Your own missions against them have been no more successful than those supervised by Karl."

A contrite Karl, "Forgive me Count Orlok."

Orlok gives a pitying look to Karl. Orlok gives few gifts, but he will spare the odd pitying look. "No. Do not rebuke yourself Karl. Like a patient father, I forgive you." Orlok offers his gesture of benediction to Karl.

More tapestries and objects d'art exit the room. Tea sets,

paintings, a porcelain milk-maid in baby blue, these all leave. Other objects enter still wrapped in the cloth that protects them in what must be their long storage. Brown-shirted men distribute them throughout the study, placing or hanging them as geometry demands.

Count Orlok, "Still, something must be done. The quinquennial meeting of our Order is almost upon us. The brethren will soon descend in mass. It would not do for them to tour the village and become embroiled with our," Orlok searches for the right word, "cowardly advisories. They might suffer," still more searching for still fewer words, "embarrassments." Orlok makes a difficult decision. "We must cancel the village tours."

A shocked Karl answers, "But they so love the tours! They come for the tours!"

Orlok waves a dismissive hand—a particular gift of his, "They come for the spectacle. They come for the rituals. They come for the investitures, the inaugurations, the echelons, the ranks, the titles, the honors of the Order. They come for the fellowship." He sighs, "They come for the beer." Orlok shudders slightly at this last.

Dr. Damarung has his own list, "They come to hail the Sacred Relic! They come to find a Suitable Vessel already in place for the Blood of the Beast! They come to bring forth the Final Resolution and to glory in the Advent of the Fourth Reich!"

Count Orlok, "Yes, yes." Another practiced dismissive wave, "And they leave their donations. We must not neglect our fiscal priorities."

Around Orlok the brown-shirted men unveil the new objects of appreciation: a bronze statue of a giant eagle squatting on a wreath-encircled swastika. Another of a great Aryan body-builder enwreathed and clutching a sword by the blade. On a nearby table a classic pen and ink stand set with a parteiadler eagle atop the ink pot lid. Beside this, a swastika bedecked tea set. And rising behind him, still tarped, a picture to replace the portrait of Mademoiselle Guimard over the mantel of the great fireplace.

Count Orlok, "We must at all times see to our financial priorities. For all this," he sweeps his arms to indicate the room, but looking about, and seeing that his magnificent study in refinement has transformed into a Hitlerian House of Kitsch, his voice drops in dismay, "must be paid for."

Orlok recovers his sardonic and worldly disdain, and lays out his plan for the coming siege, "Karl, see that our people dust and sweep the reliquary, that it may be in best splendor for our most illustrious and generous new members of the Elect."

Doctor Damarung. "I can attend to that. I'd hoped to meditate there today."

Orlok cuts him off, "Ridiculous. You must put the laboratory into a fit manner to be toured. If we cannot have the village, then we must at least offer the most extensive tour of the Abbey."

Doctor Damarung, "The laboratory must remain as I have it! Prepared for the great event! I have every instrument already in place for the procedures!"

Orlok sighs. As King Francis had to tolerate his Leonardo Da Vinci, Count Orlok must appease his Doctor Damarung. "Very well."

Doctor Damarung pursues this new topic, "You promised to announce it." He explains to Karl, "Before the brethren, at the feast of the Gathering, the Count will announce the Great Advent."

Count Orlok impatiently cuts him off, "But until then we must prepare for the great *onslaught...*"

Behind him the new picture has risen to its position above the fireplace mantle, its covering tarp about to come off.

"...Of beer guzzling, podium pounding, chair crushing, sacrilegious, tactless, vomitous, hyper-Teutonic laggards." He faces the painting. "Our Brothers in the Order..."

The tarp falls away.

"The men of..."

We see a portrait of an all too familiar man in brown uniform, Charlie Chaplin mustache, and air of superiority.

"ODESSA!"

The portrait of Adolph Hitler.

Damarung and Karl salute the image. I think you know what kind of salute.

Orlok's face shows no sign of reverence. Rather, he looks like a man with a dreary task ahead of him upon which his future depends. Orlok heaves a heavy sigh.

Frazier University of Minds – afternoon

The plaque on the door reads: Chris Gainer – Assistant Lecturer – Department of Anthropology.

Rafe, "I only mean to say, what other kind of University could it be but one *of minds*? Does anyone graduate from a University *of feet*?" Rafe opens the door to reveal the office of Chris Gainer, eternal advanced student of anthropology.

What fills this room? Books on third-hand bookcases, stacks of papers on top of stacks of other papers. A cheap desk under a full bulletin board, and two chairs risky to sit in. All typical of departmental budget priorities for over-stayed graduate students. Rafe and Natasha enter the room.

Natasha, "I detect foul play."

Rafe, "He's just a messy reader. Search for clues."

Rafe heads straight to the bulletin board on the assumption that it should hold the bulletins. In the midst of the bulletin board's chaos of thumb-tacked papers, one stands out for having a large X drawn through it. Rafe examines that one while Natasha looks at the titles of books on the shelves. Chris's books run the gamut from highly technical treatises on cultural anthropology, to more accessible works in history and culture. Natasha pulls out one now newly relevant to her in light of Janet's information: *A History of Immigration to the Argentine*.

Rafe, "Hello. What have we here?"

What we have here: a paper of scribbled in messy handwritten notes, crossed out with a large X, which says:

Otusia Facts

Afr/Mar

Ethnograph cargo cult co-evo cult shock

Chart altiplano

Take 10/1932

First contact: K Attler 1959

See Bruer and Hoffman Pro. Soc. Cult. Ant. v.107 no 3.

Rafe removes the paper and puts it on the desk. Next to it he places Halftrain's briefing document so as to make a proper study.

Flipping through the Argentine immigration book, Natasha notes its more striking pictures. One a photo of men giving a stiff-arm salute.

Rafe, "I have it now. Look at this." Natasha glances at the desk.

Rafe points to *Otusia*, "*Out to sea*. A fact Chris established."

He points to *Afr/Mar*, "*Afraid for Marcy*. Of course he would be."

He points to *ethnograph cargo cult co-evo*, "She has been *carted away by a cult*, a *completely evil* cult, which plans to shock her!"

None of this impresses Natasha, "More toys."

Rafe, "Fine. I'll decode this, you thumb through—" He glances at the book on the table, "*The Proceedings of the Society of Cultural Anthropology*. We see who gets there first."

Natasha shrugs and reads her Argentine immigration book.

Rafe will not let an obstinate partner ruin a run of good detection, "They chartered an alternate airplane. So an air charter company—best way to get a kidnapped victim out to sea. *Take*. Marcy's been taken. No kidding. No. This shows *where* she's been taken. To find that we must first contact *K. Attler*." Rafe losses steam a bit. "And then see *Bruer* and see *Hoffman* ... lots of numbers ... and a Professional Ant Cult.

Shocking."

Natasha, "Hopeless."

Rafe springs to the phone, "What am I thinking? We have the entire resources of Interpol's Communications Directorate at our disposal." He dials numbers. He hesitates. "Do you recall—"

Natasha, "301-529-3343. Extension 4325. Security code 555."

Rafe dials away, "How do you...?"

Natasha, "Trained photographic memory."

On the other end of the phone emerges the voice of the Interpol Comm Officer, "Interpol communications officer. What is your personal identification number?"

Rafe, "Uh. Would that be the same as my Social Security number?"

"No sir."

Rafe, "Would the first digit be ... one?"

"Sir I can't answer questions like that."

Rafe, "Can you tell me how many digits I have?"

"Sir?"

Rafe tries Natasha, "Personal ID Code?"

Natasha, "Yours or mine?"

That takes Rafe aback, "Well, mine."

Natasha, "20489-334-217908-0043-6"

Rafe speaks into the phone, "Two ... uh ... wait ..." Rafe holds the phone up to Natasha.

Natasha, "0489-334-217908-0043-6"

Rafe takes the phone down and claps his hand over the receiver, "Fine, but what's my master card number?"

Natasha, "404—" Rafe holds his hand up to stop her.

Interpol Comm Officer, "What can we do for you today Agent Riley?"

Rafe, "I want you to enter some names into the data base. *Attler*, two *t*'s and first name starts with a *K*. Also, *Bruer*, and *Hoffman*. I want you to cross-check these with charter plane companies. Also, cults. And kidnappings. Maybe ants. Evil. In general, I guess. Also, evil specific to cults and kidnapping."

Interpol Comm Officer, "I'm getting way too many hits sir."

Rafe to Natasha, "We have lots of hits already. I'm making serious progress here." To the Comm Officer, "I have numbers too. I have the numbers: 10/19321959107. Also, the number 3, but you may need to subtract that from the seven."

"Sir?"

Rafe, "Just use the digits. Find any connection."

Natasha, "Have you perhaps noticed the giant X through the paper?"

Rafe, into phone, "Also the letter X."

Natasha, "No, I mean X like crossed out."

Rafe, to Natasha, "X marks the spot. Found this middle of the board, not the waste-can."

Comm Officer, "Well sir, I found a small charter plane company run by a B. Hauser that matches, uh, some of your numbers. Located in Palacia Mexico."

Rafe sits bolt upright in his chair, "Give me the phone number."

Rafe holds the phone up to Natasha's ear while the Comm Officer rattles off the phone number. Natasha uses her finger to hang up the phone and punch in the new number. Rafe puts the phone to his ear.

Natasha walks the room. She pulls a book on Germanic cults from a shelf and flips through it while hearing Rafe in the background.

Rafe, "Mr. Hauser. Fine. I'm looking for a flight chartered by a Mr. Bruer or Mr. Hoffman. Or possibly a Mr. Cargo. Or maybe a cargo *flight*. But with passengers. Perhaps through Buenos Aires."

Natasha flips through the book. She sees pictures of mystic symbols and hand-signs. Among them such gestures as *pinky to chin with bird-beak sign with two finger lift*, and *three fingers out with two tucked to chest*, and also *index finger to temple and middle to cheek with downward facing bird-beak sign.* Apparently, one could not practice ariosophy without considerable finger dexterity.

Rafe, "My first contact would be K Attler. Yes. Of course. Yes, K Attler that's right. *Of course* I'm a brother. I have all the proper documents. I just..." Rafe crumples papers from the desk into the receiver. "I've just lost the paper with the date and time of departure on it." Rafe shoots a very-pleased-with-himself smile at Natasha. She shrugs. Rafe takes notes, "Right. Got it. And that takes off, as usual, from ... right. Yes sir." Then a puzzle, "Uh. Guten Tag to you too." Rafe hangs up the phone. A man triumphant.

Rafe, "While you've been wasting your time looking at books, I have found the next step. And the magic phrase turns out to be: K Attler."

Natasha slams the book closed.

Brothers of Mercy Asylum – Budapest – morning

Clearly an old and ill kept structure, built to last in the nineteenth century but just barely lasting now. The main room houses the inmates as they entertain themselves playing cards or reading books. All the inmates are peaceful and polite. They show no signs of illness or lunacy. The only distinguishing feature of the inmates: hair. Hair covers every one of them from head to foot; a comb salesman's paradise.

Trevor walks among them, rather ill at ease in the company these people covered in hair. Kip accompanies him, sporting a handle-bar moustache (his latest creation). Between them walks Dr. Hoffbrau, head of the asylum. Dr. Hoffbrau wears the same antiquated lab coat favored by Dr. Damarung. He speaks in the same guttural German accent, and he oozes the same level of deep and abiding compassion.

Trevor, "Are they dangerous?"

Dr. Hoffbrau, "Filth of course. But safe. Passive even. I don't see why you need to inspect my correspondence."

Kip, "Irregularities. At Odessa Labs we run a tight ship, and your letters have not been ship-shape."

Dr. Hoffbrau, "*Tight ship. Ship-shape.* Americanisms. You are American?"

Kip, "Odessa spans the globe. This asylum reports to a worldwide organization."

Dr. Hoffbrau, "I know. So we must all speak English now. So many Americans."

Kip wanders too far, "Under current expansion plans, we'll all be speaking Chinese soon."

Dr. Hoffbrau stops in his tracks and looks at Kip with an expression somewhere between confused and aghast. A little girl, covered in thick hair, takes Trevor's hand to offer him a toy. Trevor nearly jumps out of his skin. He takes the toy and nods to the girl.

Trevor, "Sorry dear." To Dr. Hoffbrau, "I'm rather sensitive about hair."

Dr. Hoffbrau starts walking again. The girl falls in behind them, following them as they walk.

Trevor, "What ails them?"

Dr. Hoffbrau, "A form of hypertrichosis. Viral in nature. An unusual disorder. Hair of course. Psychological timidity, pheromonal sensitivity. Nothing really interesting in itself. We work for the future of mankind, not for these creatures." Dr. Hoffbrau shoos away a hairy little boy who approaches, "We do not keep them here. We bring the rats in, extract fluids, run tests, make observations. We send all this to Dusseldorf. In good order!"

Kip goes fishing, "All for proper distillation at our lab."

Dr. Hoffbrau lowers his voice, "And then reinjected into our special patients. And all thoroughly documented with the new samples returned."

Now Trevor goes fishing, "But you do keep a record of the formulas, I dare say?"

Dr. Hoffbrau pokes his finger into Trevor's chest, "We record everything. And send it by courier. To Dusseldorf and to Doctor Damarung."

Kip, "Well of course Doctor Damarung."

Trevor, "And of course Formula XOX as well."

Dr. Hoffbrau, "Formula XOX must be well past being written down by now. I dare say no one could write it down now." He chuckles at the thought. Kip and Trevor manage a bit of a chuckle themselves, just to put things over. A pall of suspicion crosses the countenance of Dr. Hoffbrau, "My private lab lies just down this hall. But first." Dr. Hoffbrau pointedly raises his index finger to his chin, presses his middle finger to his thumb to form a bird-beak and raises his remaining fingers, pinky under the ring finger.

Trevor stares, puzzled, but expectant. Kip just stairs. Frustrated, Dr. Hoffbrau drops his hand and makes the gesture again. Kip scratches his chin.

Dr. Hoffbrau, "I'm sorry gentlemen. I can't help you." Dr. Hoffbrau shows them the exit.

At the barn of the Horowitz farm – Argentina

A clear and beautiful day at a farmyard like the others. Chris holds Katrina in her usual on the hip position. Katrina looks intently at anything her dad takes an interest in, and right now he shows interest in what lies just ahead of them. Chris walks toward it, looking at it closely, with an expression somewhere between curious and concerned. The voices of Marcy and Mr. Horowitz fade in the wind behind him.

Marcy, "So I'm asking, would you definitely describe the event as entirely natural."

Mr. Horowitz, "Well it's natural that chickens torn apart should die."

Chris and Katrina stare as Chris walks toward the sight of his concern: a barn wall, painted white. Someone has put a new coat of paint on the barn, but in the light as it hits the barn wall now, you can make out something painted underneath the new layer of white.

A large black swastika.

Chris studies the design.

Katrina, "Broken spider."

Chris, "Do you think that Mr. Horowitz painted a broken spider on his barn?" Katrina does not know much about these things, but she does not think that Mr. Horowitz likes broken spiders. Chris puts Katrina down.

Katrina, "Look for clues, Daddy?"

Chris, "Look for clues."

She runs off. Chris looks to his left and sees, standing off about ten yards, Ezra, watching him. Looking past Ezra, Chris sees the mountain monastery in the hazy distance.

Marcy stands with Mr. Horowitz and Papa Cohen by the remains of the Horowitz chicken coop. Not much coop left. Demolished really.

Marcy, "I'm just wondering if you would characterize the *event* as normal?"

Mr. Horowitz, "Normal for lately. Except it came from above." Papa Cohen looks up with concern.

Marcy, "And how would you characterize *it*?"

Mr. Horowitz shrugs, "As you say. An event."

Marcy, "But a natural event."

Mr. Horowitz shrugs.

Marcy, "Perhaps your coop suffered from a downburst?"

Mr. Horowitz, "What is a downburst?"

Marcy, "A low level wind phenomenon that blows radially from all directions. They've been known to crash planes on takeoffs and landings."

Mr. Horowitz, "Do they eat chickens?"

Chris makes his way around the barn. Katrina brings him a haul of feathers and drops them at his feet.

Katrina, "Feathers Daddy!"

Chris bends down. He picks up a small white feather to show Katrina—vocabulary building time.

Chris, "Chicken feather." He picks up a very different feather, "Eagle feather."

Katrina looks impressed.

Chris, "Big eagle feather."

Katrina agrees.

Brothers of Mercy Asylum – Budapest – night

Kip and Trevor have returned for a night visit to the asylum. They walk through its main room, now bereft of company. They scan the room with flashlights and creep softly to the private lab of Dr. Hoffbrau. Additionally, they continue an earlier dispute.

Kip, "Then I'll look for them all by myself."

Trevor, "Look for what?"

Kip, "No, you're not interested."

Trevor, "Oh tell me the bloody warning if you must."

Silence.

But Kip cannot resist, "Beware viscous attaché ant molars." He pauses for effect.

Trevor, "Fortunate you said something. We will both need to keep eyes peeled for that. You remain alert to the possible presence of ants, presumably gigantic ones if we are to beware of them. I'll inspect behind every object for signs of their luggage. Patent absurdity."

They arrive at an office marked Private Laboratory. Or rather, in German: *Privates Labor*. Kip checks under the door frame, presumably for ant molars. Trevor turns the handle and swings the door open. With caution, and with Kip alert to dentulous ants, they enter the private lab of Dr. Hoffbrau. From what little they can see in the beams of light: a desk, some shelves with beakers and bottles, a cage. Just charity asylum private lab stuff.

They enter. Kip on the side of the bottle shelves, Trevor next to the cage. Both keep flashlight beams trained on the desk. Something moves at Trevor from the cage at his right. He screams and jumps.

Trevor, "Ahhhh!!"

Kip jumps too and knocks bottles on the floor. Several break. Nothing appears to have actually attacked Trevor.

Kip, "So what do you call that? Your professional cat-burglar battle cry?"

Trevor, "You needn't have launched yourself into the furnishings."

Trevor's flashlight reveals a short, feeble, hairy-gorilla-man squatting inside the cage. The inmates at the asylum that Kip and Trevor encountered in the light of day looked and acted like people covered in hair, as indeed they were. This man has a more animal aspect and appears to be mute, or very shy indeed. He must be hungry as well. He gently holds out his hand, begging.

Trevor, "Poor fellow. Is it a fellow? What is it?"

Kip, "Sinister indeed. Interpol knew what they were doing sending us on this mission."

Trevor, "Really? I was coming to the opposite conclusion."

Kip steps to the desk, turns on a desk light, and begins to jimmy the desk drawer with a letter opener. In the better but still dim light, Trevor watches him. In the cage, behind Trevor, the hairy-gorilla-man sniffs the air. He begins to shake and twitch. His body rattles. His muscles stretch. He grows larger. His face becomes more gorilla than man.

Trevor starts to bend an ear around to better make out these new sounds in the room. The hairy-gorilla-man grunts. Trevor turns around. Trevor sees the hairy-gorilla-man—now very much more gorilla than man, so let's just admit the obvious and call him *gorilla-man*.

Gorilla-man, "Oooh! Oooh! Oooh!"

Trevor looks shocked and terrified at the sight of this new gorilla face. The gorilla-man's hands reach out and grab Trevor. It pulls Trevor twice, hard, headfirst, into the cage, then it drops him to the floor. From Trevor's rather hazy point of view from the floor, he sees Kip's head move into view, his face amazed.

Kip, "Wow!"

And with that, Trevor's view slowly fades to black.

Letters – 1995-2003

From: Father Zsolt Szarka, Brothers of Mercy Asylum, Budapest, HU, August 1, 1995.

To: Dr. Damarung, Research Assistant, Odessa/Biomax Laboratories, Dusseldorf, DE.

Dear Dr. Damarung,

I write to you in response to your recent letter. I am indeed an expert on the subject of lycanthropy and were-wolfism. I fear, however, that you have misconceived the nature of this expertise. I am not a scholar of what one might call *actual* lycanthropy. I study and write on the myths and beliefs around this idea. I came to this field of study through my encounters with certain persons who often come to our sanctuary of healing here in Budapest. I hasten to add, however, that these persons are not werewolves, nor do they suffer from anything that might be described as "lycanthropy." They certainly are not "a stronger animal/human hybrid," and I really cannot comment on their capacity to "bear the burden of foundational transplantation" as I cannot even guess what that might be. Perhaps I might offer a brief explanation.

Some of those coming to our place of healing are very hairy persons, or as we have come to prefer calling them, persons of hair. They suffer from, or very often endure with good cheer, the condition of hypertrichosis. This condition causes hair to grow on virtually every part of their bodies. While many find this an unwelcome affliction, they are much more vexed by the prejudice of others toward them than by any difficulty attending the condition in itself.

It was this fact that led me to study the mythology of werewolves. In my view the fear of werewolves stems from the once unrecognized phenomenon of serial murder committed by the morally deranged. Out of ignorance of this uncommon phenomenon of psychotic murders, common folk in these and other regions fixed upon the idea that brutal and pointless killings must stem from beasts in the form of men. Wolves proved the ideal example of a common and dangerous beast, while, to their great misfortune, persons of hair have been unjustly assumed to be the natural wolf/man form of such dangers. I have dedicated my life to aiding these poor, unfortunate persons. In pursuit of this goal I answer every letter I receive on "lycanthropy" so as to enlighten the public on these matters.

I hope that you will find this missive helpful. I cannot stress enough the importance that leading men of science such as yourself have in spreading this message of understanding.

Sincerely,

Father Szarka, Brothers of Mercy Asylum, Budapest, HU.
August 1, 1995.

From: Father Szarka, Medical Director, Brothers of Mercy Asylum, Budapest, HU, December 18, 1997.
To: Dr. Damarung, Senior Researcher, Odessa Laboratories, Dusseldorf, DE.

Dear Dr. Damarung,

It is with great joy and gratitude that we at the Brothers of Mercy Asylum received the latest financial contribution from Odessa Laboratories. We know that we have you to thank for it. It will do so much good for our patients! As you suggested, and as per the contingencies on the grant, we have put the money into medical research into hypertrichosis here at our new laboratory. To think we have a laboratory now! We have also greatly increased our admittance of persons of hair as you requested. This is all so much more than I would have dreamed of when I answered your first letter of inquiry. God truly moves in mysterious ways.

On the matter of "specimens." First, we are most happy to hear that the blood and tissue samples we have sent are proving so useful in your research (although I must again caution you against calling it "research into lycanthropy"). Second, we will, of course, send more, as per our grant agreement. Third, and I do not mean to make too strong a point of this, but I must again stress that "specimen" can only refer to blood and tissue samples, not, as your correspondence might uncharitably be taken to suggest, to the persons of hair offering the samples. These are our *patients*.

Also, while we do not doubt the therapeutic soundness of the procedure, we really must strenuously object to the suggestion that we "reinject" the "distilled viral essence" of "lycanthropy" back into what you persist in calling our "stage one were-beasts." Contrary to what your last letter seemed to suggest, this is all the more because of, not in spite of, the serum's "heightened animal DNA load." We Brothers of Mercy lack the scientific knowledge to quite know what that means, but our consensus view is that it argues against your program of "reinjection." Also, and with the deepest respect, it is not a matter of the physical act of injection (so that, *no*, "straps and chains" would not suffice) but rather of informed consent.

In light of all this we do admit that things have grown rather beyond our ken on the "medical end" as you put it. So we have all agreed to accept your kind offer to send one Dr. Hoffbrau to "get things in order." We look forward to all working together for the future of humanity.

Sincerely,

Father Szarka, Medical Director, Brothers of Mercy Asylum. December 18, 1997.

From: Farther Szarka, Assistant Researcher, Brothers of Mercy Asylum, Budapest, HU, December 18, 1999.
To: Dr. Damarung, Research Director, Odessa Laboratories, Dusseldorf, DE.

Dear Dr. Damarung,

I offer you greetings from all the Brothers. Unfortunately, as I have mentioned to you before, this number grows increasingly small. I do not ascribe this attrition in our numbers to your preferred theory that we "fail to breed." I fear you misunderstand the nature of our vows.

Rather, I attribute our recent wave of resignations to the activities of your "acolyte" Dr. Hoffbrau. With great reluctance we acceded to his demand for a private lab. Would that we had shown yet more reluctance! I do not pretend to understand such concepts as "third stage were-beastism," "active pheromonal discharge," "morphological scent sensitivity," "hyper bite-transmissibility," "lycanthropic durability," or "hybridized mammal/avian DNA reinjection." Nor do I wish any of this explained to me! It does not help in the least to replace "viral extract" with "formula X" and "DNA hybrideal fluid" with "formula XO." We Brothers of Mercy still fail to understand you in the same disturbing manner. Furthermore, the growing presence of this terminology here at the asylum has disheartened our Order and lead to a vast migration of brothers from what had been dedicated service to the relief of suffering.

Well can I understand that a man of science like yourself might find our Order behind the times and even obsolete. Perhaps our troubled souls do not move you. But think of the persons of hair. They come seeking comfort and treatment (or increasingly the "grant money" Dr. Hoffbrau distributes), but they do not receive the love and acceptance that we Brothers of Mercy made central to our healing mission. Though we have never met, I know you must be a decent man given all you have done for the asylum. (Have you actually met Dr. Hoffbrau?!? I cannot believe that you have.) I plead with you to do something.

And I fear that soon I will need to do more than plead. To speak frankly, and I trust confidentially (I do not trust Dr. Hoffbrau with this), some persons of hair have gone missing. Entrusted to our asylum, they have failed to return to their families. I do not know where they are. If something cannot be done soon I will be forced to go to the authorities. I'm sure you do not want this. It would be an embarrassment to the asylum. Ever reliant on your judgement and generosity, I cannot but put my faith in you.

Confident in your aid,

Father Szarka, Brother of Mercy. December 18, 1999

From: Dr. Hoffbrau, Director, Brothers of Mercy Asylum, Budapest, HU, July 7, 2003.

To: Dr. Damarung, Creator of the Suitable Vessel, ODESSA, Kehlsteinhausdorf, AG.

Dear Fritz,

I am pleased to report that all aspects of the Brothers of Mercy Asylum have been "regularized." All personnel have been vetted or eliminated. All records have been secured. All correspondence now proceeds by courier. I will continue to deliver samples to Odessa Laboratories. I will forward specimens to your facility and limit reinjection experiments to those in early second stage.

All Glory to the Final Resolution!

Sincerely,

Your dear friend, Heidrick.

Hotel room – Budapest – day

A nice enough room; old fashioned. Trevor probably picked this one. Kip sits studying documents. Trevor holds an icebag to his head. Trevor has pretty much had it with studying documents. Silence prevails.

Kip, "Clearly, *beware viscous attaché ant molars* made no sense."

Silence.

Kip, "In retrospect I think Halftrain must have meant *beware vicious attack animals*."

Trevor says nothing.

Kip inspects documents, "You know, I think we've been going about this all wrong."

Trevor, "I am amazed. Stunned. Definitely stunned. But I mean to say that I am astounded. You have managed that revelation without a single blow to the head. Unfelled by impact and unscathed by concussion, you have discovered that some fundamental error infects all our efforts. Do tell, old boy, do tell."

Kip ignores Trevor's pique—no one denies he has taken the blows on this one—and presses his point, "It's all about the courier. The man in the gray fedora. Every lead we find he shows up. Documents to deposit. And now we're one step ahead of him. He'll be picking up documents from the asylum. He'll have to take the river path back from the asylum. We jump him there. We obtain the documents straight from the courier."

Trevor lowers the ice bag, "You have something there. But not jump him. I've had quite enough *jumpings*, thank you very much, not to mention the possibility of witnesses on so public a path by the Danube."

Kip, "What then?"

Trevor stands. He pulls Kip into position in front of him and takes an envelope from the desktop.

Trevor, "I pick his pocket, rather a specialty, and hand off to you." He slips the envelope into Kip's hands, demonstrating proper technique. "With a little practice I can make a decent bag-capture man of you in no time. You'll have his goods in your hands, and the man in the gray fedora will be none the wiser."

Kip nods excitedly, "Fantastic. I'll notify headquarters on the Lector."

Trevor groans and replaces the icebag on his head.

Charter plane office – Mexico – night

Rafe and Natasha stand at the corner of the small, nondescript building. Rafe wears a nicely fitted suit with waistcoat. Natasha wears a black dress fitted to show her figure while concealing her standard attire of form-fitting kick-your-ass spy-wear. They watch the door of the charter office. From that door one need only walk fifty yards to the charter plane, its engines already idling, airstairs pulled up to the door. They watch two men make that trip from the office to the plane. These men are dressed as monks. Brown robes and raised cowls obscure them completely. The monks board the plane.

Rafe talks to Natasha while they watch the office, "Palacia. Town in Mexico."

Natasha ignores him.

Rafe, "That plane, the flight goes to Buenos Aries."

Nothing.

Rafe, "The man on the phone got very excited about *K Attler*."

Natasha, "I grant you Buenos Aries—but I do not think this *Attler* means a man's name."

Rafe, "I understand you have some theories derived from books, but I brought us here based on hard, sound, logic. And a careful attention to documents. Authentic handwritten documents from one of the people we look to find. So properly sourced. Not books published for any Tom, Dick and Harry to read."

Natasha looks confused, "You have more names of men?"

Rafe, "No. A colloquialism. Antiquated now probably."

Natasha, "So not new clues, these men Tom and Dick?"

Rafe, "No! Common names. As in just anyone could read a book. My point being that while you look for enlightenment in books anyone might read, I have based our investigation on documents particular to the case. I have found the secret networks from the breadcrumbs pinned on a bulletin board. I've fitted the puzzle-pieces back into the maze. I've followed the tracks into the labyrinth. I've connected the dots to make the lightbulb go off. I've followed the red herring. I've proven the paradox. I've staged a eureka moment. A Copernican revolution. A triple-word score. X marked the spot and I brought us to X."

Natasha, "Or perhaps we shoot the wild goose."

Rafe, "Chase. You chase the wild goose." He looks at her.

"You're having me on, aren't you?"

Natasha smiles slightly. She nods ahead of them, "Monks have boarded. We go now."

They walk to the office door, passing under a sign: ODESSA CHARTERS. They enter the small office. Before them sits a man behind a desk. He is Herr Hauser. Stout, bald, thick-necked, bent over his work: that's Herr Hauser. His desktop nearly bows with the weight of invoices, reservations, and copies of identity papers. Behind him you can see a small room. If you, like Natasha, were to examine that room carefully, you would see monks' habits hung in a closet.

Rafe sets to work on Herr Hauser, "Hello. Hola. Klein and Kraus. Here for the plane." Hauser looks unimpressed. Rafe presses on, "We spoke on the phone."

Natasha inspects the desk. The papers lie upside down to her, but memorizing upside-down documents poses no challenge for Russian trained spies. It's like a day two lesson at Russian spy school.

Herr Hauser notices something about Natasha, "A woman?"

Rafe, "Where? Oh. Yes. Klein. I'm Kraus. So should we just board, or what's the process?"

Natasha flips pages off of other pages to see names. Hauser moves the stack.

Herr Hauser, "I must see your documents."

Rafe, "Lost. Accident. You might say they are—" He leans in to impart a secret, "Out to Sea." Rafe leans back. He nods. Say no more.

Herr Hauser, "I'm sorry. I can't help you."

Rafe, "Would it make a difference if we knew the old cape routine?"

No, it would not help.

Natasha, "We have orders from C.T. Orlok."

This gets Hauser's attention; Rafe's too. Hauser instinctively places a hand over the papers before him.

Rafe races to exploit the opening, and, frankly, to catch up, "And Mr. Cargo."

Herr Hauser, "What?"

Rafe, "Not to mention Doctor Damarung." Herr Hauser straightens. Rafe carries on, "We meet him at the coast." A bit confusing that, but Hauser almost believes.

Herr Hauser, "Very well. One more thing." Hauser places an index finger on his chin, makes a bird-beak of his second finger and thumb while lifting the other two digits, pinky under third finger.

Rafe smiles.

Herr Hauser waits.

Natasha raises her hand to her chest, three fingers out, two tucked to her chest.

Here Hauser, "No. That is not correct."

Natasha, "Then what of..." She places her index finger on her chin, middle finger on her cheek while using the others against her thumb to make a downward facing bird-beak form.

Herr Hauser, "I'm afraid it's too late now."

Natasha, "What of this one..." She roles her fingers together, pinky first, till all form a fist. Then she hits him in the jaw, knocking him out.

Rafe. "Did I miss a meeting?"

Natasha, "Drag him into office. Tie him." She rips out the phone line to use as rope. (Phones used to be connected to walls by "lines" that you could redeploy as ropes with which to tie people up—one of their charms really. Let's just say that cell phones can't do everything the old land-lines could do.) Rafe drags Hauser.

Rafe, "And how do we get on the plane now?"

Natasha pulls out two monk's robes from the closet, "Make dot connection."

On the Danube path – Budapest – night
Budapest frames the river boardwalk. Old-World

architecture rises above the calm waters flowing below classic bridges. Hardly a sex-shop in sight. Kip and Trevor stand on the side of the path looking out for the courier in the gray fedora. Trevor wears a classic British trench coat. Kip wears glued on mutton chops. Not Elvis sideburns but Martin Van Buren mutton chops. Kip and Trevor both look down the boardwalk.

Kip, "Definitely mentions the courier."

Nothing from Trevor.

Kip, "Regionally correct too, if you ask me."

Trevor sighs and humors him, "Very well."

Kip leans in to share this latest intelligence from headquarters, *"Beware: courier is a Croatian expatriate."*

Trevor motions to the fedora wearing man approaching, "Do your job and his nationality will hardly enter into matters." They split up. Trevor walks ahead of the courier while Kip falls in behind him. Trevor stops, as if remembering something. He turns and with perfect timing brushes against the courier.

Trevor, "Sorry." Trevor brushes Kip as the courier heads on his way.

Kip drops the package. Pages blow in the wind past the courier, who very much notices. The courier turns, checking his pocket.

Kip, "Grab the papers!" Kip charges the courier. The fedora man takes a classic karate pose and lands a karate punch in Kip's stomach with a "Kiiiaaa!"

Kip doubles over.

Trevor approaches the courier who takes the karate pose. The courier launches a spinning kick. "Kiiiiiaaaaa!" He kicks Trevor in the head, spinning him round and knocking him out.

Kip nails the courier in the back of the head, taking him out. Kip sees Trevor, down for the count, "Oh boy." Documents fly into the Danube as Kip hoists Trevor onto his shoulders once again.

Andean mountain path – Argentina – day

A pleasant day and a long hike. Papa Cohen leads, Chris, carrying Katrina, walks beside Marcy. Hadassah, Ehud, and Ezra hang back behind them. Marcy talks with Chris.

Marcy, "I feel like they don't want to tell me anything."

Chris, "Maybe you don't ask the right questions."

Marcy, "I should ask about seventh sons?"

Chris, "You should know a little about the culture you visit on *my* working vacation."

Marcy, "I'm sorry. I tried to kill two birds with one stone."

Chris does his best Marcy imitation, which, to be fair, sounds spot on, "Oh Chris, I've found this wonderful undocumented group in the Andes you might study."

Marcy, "Together, that's what I thought."

Chris, "I had a perfectly good prospect lining up in Mauritania."

Marcy, "I *meant* this to be *mostly* your thing."

Chris, "And you would look after … The Dumpling."

Katrina, "No dumpling. Crunchy candy."

Behind them Hadassah laughs to herself. Marcy takes The Dumpling to carry. She looks back at Hadassah and the Cohen brothers.

Marcy, "Everyone understands English."

Chris, "Common in Argentina."

Marcy, "But they don't say anything with it."

Chris, "Your executive mentality shows. You can't treat this as a staff meeting with agenda items to tick off. You need to coax a little. Find a few things yourself. Build a little trust."

Marcy, "Do they want us to know or not?"

Chris, "Maybe they do, but they don't want to tell us."

Marcy, "Why not?"

Chris, "Well one of us carries a badge and acts like a policeman. Maybe they know things they don't want to tell the police. Perhaps they don't want to make us accessories after the fact."

Marcy, "Fact of what?"

They walk.

Chris, "Fur. Fur that isn't fur. Lots of it."

Katrina nods.

Chris, "That footprint in the shed."

Marcy, "For which mankind can offer no earthly explanation."

Chris changes tack, "You know the Xtapa tribe do a panther dance. The shamans of the tribe; maybe the unmarried young males as well, hard to say. Understudied group. Point is, they—I mean the Xtapa shamans and such—tie paws to their feet. Creating claw feet. They dance in their panther claw feet. And maybe the young men find brides, I don't know."

Marcy, "So *they* were here? The Xtapa dancers?"

Chris, "They number less than seven hundred all told and occupy six acres in the heart of the Brazilian rainforest."

Marcy, "So not close."

Katrina, "Faaarrrrr away." Chris gives her a thumbs up.

Marcy, "Meaning what then?"

Chris, "You want a certain kind of explanation. And you can find explanations of that type if you look hard enough. But finding an explanation of the kind you seek doesn't mean you have gotten any closer to solving your mystery."

Katrina, "Terror in den Bergen!"

Hadassah smiles behind them.

Marcy, "So because I don't see the relevance of paw-feet, and giant feathers, and great mounds of unidentifiable fur-hair, of any of it, to the issue of night attacks and torn to shred alpacas, then I have to accept Xtapa shaman paratroops. I'm stuck with naturalistic but blindingly implausible explanations or...?" She shrugs.

Little Katrina intones with menace, "Werewolves."

They crest a hill and before them they see, framed by darkening clouds, on its mountain top, the monastery. They stop to look.

Marcy, "Kloster Adler."

Chris nods, "In all of its anachronistic glory."

Marcy, "Abbey of the Eagles."

Chris, "Good name. German. Not native to the area though. Eagles I mean."

Marcy presses on with some reluctance, "The tracks lead back to it. Human tracks. And from it. Maybe wolf tracks."

Chris, "Also not native. Size issue too."

Marcy, "The Cohens clearly don't care for the place."

Chris, "And they don't seem like sit-by-and-wait type of people. But maybe they need just a little official cover."

Marcy, "Someone with a badge."

Chris, "And a heart of gold."

Marcy agrees. She takes the plunge, "So, just go knock on the door?"

Chris looks over at the Cohens, gathered at a distance and watching, "Let's see what the locals think."

Chris and Marcy look back to the monastery, now God-lit through the clouds, a promise to all mankind.

Marcy, "You know I figured out the abbey angle at the second farm. When did you get it?"

Katrina covers her eyes.

Chris, "Gift shop."

Hotel room – Budapest – day

Trevor wears a wet cloth on his head. He meditates on the blessings, and limits, of aspirin. He reviews his life for key mistakes. Early ones. The ones whose correction could have really made a difference. He has a list of topics, well known by his colleague, to which he does not wish to return. They are the topics which prove irresistible.

Kip walks on egg-shells. Still, he can't resist, "I don't think Halftrain meant that the courier was a Croatian expatriate."

This astounds Trevor, "Really? Only now? I deduced that the moment before his foot hit my head. I said to myself, *Good god man, he's not Croatian at all!*"

Point taken. Kip deduces that this may be a sore subject with Trevor. He tries a more analytical approach, "We didn't recover any documents. One might think we've run out the line."

Trevor, "One might think that, if one's head were not split in two."

Kip, "We've hit a dead end."

Trevor, "Please do not say *hit*."

Kip can't be entirely sure, but signs hint that Trevor may be losing his zest for the hunt. Keeping a stiff upper lip proves difficult when the world continues to pound one's skull into one's jaw.

But as always, Trevor recovers himself, "Wait a moment. I've had a brainstorm. Or a hemorrhage. No, a brainstorm." Trevor pops up, only dizzy for a moment, and retrieves documents from the desk and lays them across the table. He begins his explanation, "Here we see documents from von Richter's safe, and here from that horrid exploding thing at the laboratory."

Kip looks.

Trevor, "What do you notice?"

Kip, "Scorch marks?"

Trevor, "Looking past all that. What do they have in common?"

Kip looks, "Ink. Sorry, I wasn't ready for this exam."

Trevor, "Odessa."

Kip, "Oh."

Trevor, "Odessa Laboratories. Odessa Chemicals. Odessa Industries. They even have an air-charter company mentioned somewhere in here. Look at the letter head. Odessa Industries."

Kip, "Okay."

Trevor, "Now look at where Odessa Industries maintains its principal offices. Just read off the letterhead: *Berlin*, *Paris*, *Munich*, and some place called *Nido de Aquila*."

Kip, "Never heard of the last one."

Trevor, "Precisely! That must be the real locus of all this skullduggery. The very capital of this Empire of Crime. Could hardly be on a masthead with Berlin and Paris otherwise."

Kip, "We have a plan?"

Trevor, "Indeed we do. Fire up the old Lector, or better, look ourselves, and discover the location of this obscure hamlet."

Kip, "And then?"

Trevor, "Well, if I were looking for Formula XOX—and were I not suffering from concussive euphoria—well then I should very much like to go see this Nido de Aquila."

Kip agrees. It's so nice to see Trevor feeling better.

Within a chartered plane – midair – night

Rafe and Natasha sit uncomfortably, hooded up, in close confinement with the rowdiest bunch of monks ever to conclave in the air. The plane appears to have been converted from cargo use to passenger use with limited seating and large spaces for standing about. The monks like to stand about. Apart from slapping each other's backs, standing about appears their favorite pastime. The one supports the other really. But apart from the jolly re-introductions accompanied by vertebra damaging blows, all feels peaceful and mostly quiet. Then someone breaks out the beer. They swill it like, well, monks—Medieval German Branch. Lots of German words fly about, but principally the brothers speak the Latin of our era: English.

Rafe has made two acquaintances, seated next to him, though no one really sits much in the seats, rather they spill over into the charter plane's ample aisle. Both Rafe's new friends are fat, vulgar pieces of work—beer belly friars. They introduced themselves as Dieter and Johan. Dieter evidently works in the concrete business. Which Rafe did not know monks were even allowed to do. Johan claims to work as a fire safety inspector, although he says that he'd "rather start them." Dieter concurs with the sentiment. Rafe struggles to recall anything he ever learned of theology that might make sense of that. Mostly though, Dieter and Johan drink beer and look for backs to slap. Rafe keeps his back firmly against his seat.

A man at the front of the plane has an announcement to make. He looks to be just another monk, but his fellow members of the order refer to him as Corporal Fitz.

Corporal Fitz, "If I may have your attention." The monks quite down. Fitz continues, "If I may have you stand." They all do, some more easily than others given the cramp quarters and differing levels of inebriation. "We have crossed into international waters." Approving murmurs. "According to our ritual, we may unveil!"

The monks remove their robes. Revealing beneath: brown shirted storm trooper uniforms. Nazi arm bands and all. A general hurrah arises. "Hurrah!" Then they turn and face Rafe and Natasha, the only monks left still robed. A long pause follows.

Rafe removes his robe, the monks gasp. Natasha removes her robe, the monks make a sound very like a gasp just assaulted with a monkey-wrench, soaked in alcohol.

Dieter breaks the silence, "What the hell!?!"

Rafe puffs his chest out and speaks in full voice, that all the plane may hear him, "Gentlemen," Rafe looks about, "of the Reich. I am the Archduke Ivan Dragomiloff Kopopkin, direct descendent and heir to Archduke Kopopkin, General of the White Russians, the Terror of the Bolsheviks, and defender of..." Rafe pauses for affect, and because it is not clear of what the crowd might approve of defending, so he tries, "Womanhood." A holding action at best, but onward, "And I, like my Grand..." he checks himself, "great ..." more math, "great Grandfather; I, Archduke Kopopkin, have sworn my life ... my fortune ... my blood ... to..." To? "The cause!"

They seem impressed. Surprised, but impressed.

Johan points to Natasha, "Who is she?"

Rafe takes a deep breath, "Gentlemen. I have the honor

of presenting to you: the direct descendent of the sole survivor of the Bolshevik massacre of the Romanovs." Deep breath, "The great, great, granddaughter of the Archduchess Anastasia!" He pauses, "Gentlemen I give you Anastasia…" more math, "the Fifth!" Very dramatic pause, "Rightful Czarina of all the Russians!"

They greet his announcement in silence.

Natasha speaks, in her native tongue, *"You are strange little men with large bellies and no necks, but I greet you as Anastasia of Russia, Czarina."*

Deadly silence. Broken when Dieter hugs Natasha.

Dieter, "Anastasia!"

Cheers all around! The assembled Nazis collectively shout: "Anastasia!!!" All of them line up to give Natasha a hug. She hates it, but Rafe looks quite pleased with himself.

Letters – 1942-1989

From: SS Senior Colonel Ryker Schmitt, Nazi Party Deputy District Leader, Director of Reappropriation of Conquered Assets, Bullion and Movable Property for State Use, Reich Chancellery, Berlin, May 15, 1941.

To: SS Captain (Discharged!) Otis Orlok, Nazi Party Sub Area Leader (Expelled!), Deputy Director of Reappropriation of Conquered Assets, Bullion and Movable Property for State Use (Dismissed!), Buenos Aries, Argentina.

Dear Traitor!

You are a pig-dog and also die in pain! You have absconded with art meant for high party officials! You have stolen gold taken from legally conquered peoples! You have fled our most glorious cause at our hour of triumph! Die, coward, die!

Do not write to me of "forging a path ahead." Germany's conquering armies forge our way, invincible. Do not write of establishing "pipelines for fleeing SS members and their property." We are the SS! We do not flee! I do not care how you came to this "legacy for the German People." I spit at your "comfortable place to enjoy the fruits of our labor." I always knew you were a lazy coward. Would that you had been lazier! I want that art back! Return the gold or I will have you shot! Damn you! Do not expect to hear from me ever again! I curse you, Pig-dog!

SS Senior Colonel Schmitt. May 15, 1941.

From: SS Major Ryker Schmitt, Nazi Party Reginal Office Leader (Temporary), Assistant Deputy of Casualty Reports, Reich Chancellery (Fuhrer Bunker), Berlin, January 20, 1945.

To: SS Colonel Otis Orlok (Reinstated), Operational Head, ODESSA, Nido de Aquila, Argentina.

My Dear Otis,

It has been so long since we wrote. Too long! I hope all is well with you and your new organization. Such an evocative name. Everyone is talking about it here! Such a lovely town as well. I did so enjoy showing around the pictures you sent. And what a way you phrase it: "a resort for the master race." Very enticing. Though some of us are a bit unsure what you mean by "taking holy orders" and "joining an elect brotherhood." Aren't we already an elect brotherhood?

It was so kind of you to ask how we all are getting on. I'm sad to report that things aren't going as well here as everyone had hoped. Frankly, we have suffered the odd reverse or two. Altogether too much defeatism on German lips and too many Russian phrasebooks in German pockets. We do take measures against all that, naturally. But it seems there are some problems one can't execute one's way out of.

But let us not dwell on such melancholy thoughts! I have been asked by a collection of our old friends to say, *yes*, we would love an opportunity to make use of ODESSA "repositioning routes." Of course, we understand your considerable overhead. So every man of us will be "bringing contributions." We are all of us patriots, but everything must be paid for, as you say. Along those lines I cannot stress enough that those "joining the New Reich in the New World" expect safety, comfort and ranks commensurate with their character. But all this I'm sure you understand.

Finally, I have other interesting news that, due to its sensitive nature, I can only fully share by way of a personal courier in the near future. Let me just say here that on my end there has been some talk of an extraordinary nature. Talk that gives a glimmer of hope looking out into the longer future of our movement. Something all patriots would rally round, and something that, should you choose to handle it, would make the ODESSA escape route the premier choice of all good SS men. But more on that later.

For now let me just say what a pleasure it was to hear from you again.

Sincerely,

Your Dearest Friend, Ryker. January 20, 1945.

From: SS Captain (Secret) Ryker Schmitt, Regional Director, ODESSA, Berlin FRG, March 4, 1968.
To: SS General Alaric Orlok, Supreme Head, ODESSA, Kehlsteinhausdorf, AG.

Dear General Orlok,

I send you condolences on the recent death of your father. He was a great man. A patriot, a friend, and a businessman of visionary proportions. We will all miss him.

But let us not dwell on such melancholy thoughts. Rather let me congratulate you on your promotion to Supreme Head of our organization. We all feel relieved knowing that our safety and future still lie in the hands of an Orlok. You will, I'm sure, make your late father proud. And let me offer further congratulations on the recent birth of your son, Frederick. Quite a dynasty you have going there.

Briefly touching on another matter: your proposed budget. We here in *ODESSA Europe* completely agree with your proposal for "aggressive spending." Yes, the Abbey needs repair. Yes, you must keep yourself in a manner becoming your rank. Yes, the keeping of the Relic imposes necessary expenses. We agree with all this.

Nevertheless, your proposal would entail spending down capital reserves to a considerable degree. And while I do not mean to cast aspersions on anyone in the organization, I do think it fair to say that the years since our finest hours have slightly dimmed enthusiasm for our organization. Funding these increased expenses may prove difficult. Food for thought.

Sincerely,

Ryker Schmitt. March 4, 1968.

From: Senior Acolyte (Third Degree) Major Joseph Fuchs, Director ODESSA European Operations, Berlin, FDG, April 12, 1989.

To: General Count Frederick von Orlok, High Pontiff (Inaugurated) of ODESSA, Kehlsteinhausdorf. AG.

Dear Count von Orlok,

Condolences for your loss and congratulations on your elevation. All hail von Orlok! Meaning no insult to your father, it was time for new blood. Finances have been poor for some time. Membership falls off. It almost seems like the good old days of our grandfathers have been lost forever.

So you can imagine how excited we all were reading your letter! We wholeheartedly endorse your program to re-invigorate ODESSA with a renewed sense of purpose. Just the thing! And we were very intrigued with your suggestion on how to do this. Brilliant! It includes everything we might want. Strength! Piety! Purpose! And all based in science. Not to mention that the status quo with respect to the Sacred Relic has never been adequate. New leadership brings new ideas! All hail von Orlok!

I also concur with your thought that such a program, properly whispered in every ODESSA ear, would "shake loose some cash," as you say.

And, yes, I do think I can help with a recommendation. While I know of no established researcher ready to start your project, I do know of a young man with great promise. Smart, dedicated, racially and politically in line, and already possessed of a degree in biology (conventional, rather than racially correct biology, but good enough). Best of all he is filled with fire to do our great work. He would be thrilled with your program if you allow me to share it with him. So in aid to your effort, I include the resume of Fritz Damarung. May the two of you go forth in glory!

Sincerely,

Senior Acolyte Joseph Fuchs. April 12, 1989.

On a commercial air flight – midair – day

Seated, Trevor sips a drink, Kip peruses the latest issue of *Digilog; the Journal of Conceptual Body Art*. Kip sports no hair-based disguise.

Trevor, "You display not a whisker. No disguise? Presenting your bare countenance to the world? Unmasked? Without wool? Canvas unadorned, as it were?"

Kip, "It's a long flight. The glue itches."

Trevor, "Anything for art excepting skin irritation, eh?" Trevor takes a drink. "Can't say I mind. Glad not to be sitting next to a petit goatee, or a Van Dyke, or a Balbo, or an a la Souvarov, or a Fu Manchu, or any other hirsute monstrosity. Certainly not for eighteen hours." Trevor brushes his mustache. "All things in moderation."

On the tarmac – Buenos Aires Airport – day

The "brothers," now back in monastic habits, transition from the charter plane to the charter bus a few yards away, all in the middle of a tarmac. Rafe and Natasha walk the short distance, enrobed as before.

Rafe, "I'm thinking … just a theory here, but maybe, *nasty desiccated asthmatics* might have meant *Nazis disguised as monks*." Following the other monks, and without what any right-thinking person might describe as a chance to make a break for it, they enter the bus.

At the Cohen farm – Argentina – night

In a living room now converted into a military equipment depot, the Cohen's pack large round backpacks with supplies for a hiking trip. Chris watches, astounded at their idea of camping. The supplies include rolls of dynamite with timers and electrical detonation accessories, ammunition, a giant WWII vintage machine gun for Papa, walkie-talkies, and sandwiches.

On the sofa, Marcy talks to Miriam, the clan matriarch. Miriam holds Katrina.

Marcy, "Thank you for looking out for Katrina, we should be gone just a few days."

Miriam bounces a happy Katrina on her knee.

Miriam, "We will have great adventures in town."

Marcy pulls four letters from her bag, "Could you post these for me there? They go to friends." She reads the names to see that they are correct., "Rafe Riley, Natasha Raskalitkanof, Trevor Sinjun-Tunsby, and Kip Carson."

Miriam, "I will see to it."

Marcy looks at Chris who watches the Cohens with concern. He takes notes on a pad. Maybe this counts as an anthropology trip after all.

Papa Cohen, "Mama, where did you put the spare radio detonator?"

Maybe not.

The majestic Andes

The beautiful Andean Mountains. The vistas from high peaks. The lovely valleys. The quaint villages. Flutes and Flamenco dancing. People going about their work on farms and vineyards; feeding chickens, shepherding alpacas. Let's just take a moment to marvel at this marvelous place.

Before things get messy.

On a street – Nido de Aquila – afternoon

Kip and Trevor, kitted out in hiking gear and backpacks, stand on a rather Uber-German street across from a small building with a sign above it. The sign says: ODESSA INDUSTRIES – WORLD HEADQUARTERS. Below this sign, another: DR. BAUM – DENTIST. The ground floor of this modest building houses a gift shop. Mostly walking sticks and beer steins from the look of its window display.

Kip, "Seems very German for Argentina."

Trevor agrees, "Suspiciously Teutonic. Ominously Gothic. Frighteningly Friesian. Which I take as a good sign in light of all we've seen till now."

Kip looks about distractedly while Trevor remains all eyes on the ODESSA office.

Kip, "If they named the town Nido de Aquila, why all the signs calling it Kehlsteinhausdorf?"

Trevor, "They both mean *Village of the Eagles*. Managed to discover that without a Lector decoder, mind you."

Kip, "Still don't want to hear the warning then?"

Trevor, "Still don't."

Kip, "Very brief warning this time."

Trevor looks annoyed.

Kip, "Just two words."

Trevor, "Very well. What two words?"

Kip, "Beware Navies."

Trevor, "Excellent. I'll keep a weather eye out for any nautical threats. Although given our distance from any ocean I have some hope we have finally overcome the curse of the Lector alerts."

Looking to his right at nothing in particular, Kip sees Miriam Cohen walking towards them, carrying Katrina Gainer.

Kip, "It's funny. Wherever you go, you project the familiar onto the new. The mind creates its own reality from what it has."

Trevor, "Stop babbling, I'm trying to observe." Miriam and Katrina pass Trevor and Kip. That catches Trevor's attention. As Miriam walks past, Katrina leans back and waves at Trevor.

Trevor, "How in the name of all Adam's children?"

Miriam walks past the local dentist office. Miriam takes a shortcut to the post office down a narrow alley, Katrina riding her hip. Miriam senses people following. Her stalkers walk close behind. Almost threateningly close. Miriam spins around, drawing a pistol, a Mauser C96, classic German Brutalist design, sometimes it scares targets to death without even going off. She levels it at Kip and Trevor.

Above the gun barrel they see the eyes of Miriam Cohen, loving matriarch of the Cohen family. The look in those eyes suggest someone asking herself, *center mass or head shot*?

Katrina, "Uh oh."

Trevor attempts an explanation, "Excuse us madam. Just thought we recognized the young lady. Terrible mistake, I'm sure."

Katrina, "Hi Trevor."

Trevor, nods, "Katrina."

Miriam, "You are Trevor Sinjun-Tunsby?"

This throws Trevor, "Why, yes I am."

Miriam lowers the pistol, "I have a letter for you."

Trevor's jaw drops.

Katrina, "Hi Kip."

Kip, "Hey firecracker."

Miriam holsters the weapon and looks through her letters, "Kip Carson?"

Kip, "Yes?"

Miriam hands them each their letter.

Kip, astounded, "Argentina has one hell of a postal service."

Trevor, "It's from Marcy. She must be on the search for Formula XOX as well."

They open the letters.

Trevor, "This will blow the case wide open!"

From the envelops they pull...

Trevor, "It's a postcard." Trevor reads, *"Having a lovely time in Argentina, wish you were here."*

Kip, "Hey, mine's a picture of that clock tower we passed." Kip reads, *"Always think of you when I see something mechanical."* Kip smiles, "How sweet."

Trevor scratches at the texture of reality in a futile quest for sense, "But what does it mean? Delivered by hand, by her own child, in the middle of the Andes? *Having a lovely time?*"

Kip, "Code obviously. If we replace every *e* with an *s*—"

Trevor, "Stop! Stop this madness!"

Miriam sets aside suspicion. If the planet holds at least two harmless men, these are they.

Trevor attempts a last desperate gambit: ask a real and living person for a moment of help, "Madam. We are friends of Marcy Gainer's. Colleagues actually. Brothers in arms. I mean to say, very far from strangers." Trevor looks about for evidence. "The child knows us."

Katrina nods.

Kip, "We're on a mission. Same one as Marcy. Has to be."

Trevor, "Yes, it must be. The world can only bear so much coincidence."

Kip, "A vital mission."

Trevor, "Yes. And it would help us frightfully if you could tell us just where we might find Mrs. Gainer. She may be in a good deal of danger."

Miriam, "She travels with my husband and our children."

Trevor, "All the more. *They* may be in danger."

Miriam partly agrees, "Someone is in danger."

Trevor, "We are duty bound to aid her. If you could just tell us where she has gone."

Miriam takes the postcard from Trevor's hand. She flips it over and holds the picture up to Trevor. He sees the picture of Kloster Adler, snuggled on its mountain top.

Andean mountain side – late afternoon

Marcy, Chris, and the Cohens march to the base of a mountain. A sheer cliff rises above them. From where they stand below this cliff they can barely see a wall of Kloster Adler.

Chris, "It feels so liberating not to be a pony."

Marcy, "You should have stayed behind."

Chris, "On *my* working vacation?"

Marcy, "*I'm* the Interpol agent."

Chris, "After all this they will make *me* the police detective and *you* can write a dissertation on nappies."

Behind them Hadassah says to Ehud, in Hebrew, "*When I marry—not so much fighting.*" Ehud shudders at the thought of someone fighting with Hadassah.

Within a bus – on a mountain road – late afternoon

How many bottles of beer on this wall? And how many will remain once we have taken one down and distributed it evenly to the singing monks? At least with real beer, instead of imagined bottles, the singing would have slowed down. For fellowship's sake Rafe had thrown in on the first thirty lagers. Natasha had stood on her royal dignity and refused even one chorus. After lyrically passing around enough ale to inebriate a platoon of water-buffalo, Rafe had descended into exhausted silence, broken whenever Dieter or Johann had looked his way, at which point Rafe imitated a man jauntily catching up with the round. Rafe thought it the least the Archduke would do. He could not help, though, but be a bit annoyed that he had provided Natasha, and not himself, with royal dignity. How does she always land on her feet without saying a word?

For her part, Natasha looks out the window of the bus, bored. The bus passes two hikers, forcing them from the narrow road.

On the narrow road

Kip and Trevor hike up the road, acting on Miriam's intelligence, and, they hope, Marcy's instructions. In their hiking gear and backpacks they look the ordinary tourists. Kip walks on the outside next to the road. A bus bears down on them lilting this way and that in the great tradition of Andean bus lilting. Kip, jumping back from the bus, sees Natasha briefly through its window.

Kip, "You know, it's funny how wherever you go, you project the familiar onto the new. The mind creates its own reality from what it has."

Trevor, "Let's not start that again. I cannot endure sore feet, disheveled reality, and speculative metaphysics all at once."

Kip, "Are we there yet?"

Trevor consults the tourist map that serves as their non-Lector-based guide, "We have almost arrived."

Kip, "But how do we get in?"

Trevor, "In our own fashion. With stealth my good man, with stealth."

Kip and Trevor crest the hill and see before them a modest building from which cable car lines ascend to a destination high up the mountain.

Inside the lower cable car room – late afternoon

A functional space for the cable car which runs up from the high side of the valley to the mountain fastness of Kloster Adler.

A cable car mechanic ushers monks, Rafe and Natasha among them, into the large but soon cramped cable car. The monks stand shoulder to shoulder and cheek to considerable jowl. With a jolt the cable car begins to move. Looking out the window in front of her, Natasha can see they have a long journey up.

As the cable car begins its ascent, Kip and Trevor leap

from the roof of the cable car housing onto the top of the cable car. A feat all by itself, they have also done it in silence and with minimal disturbance to the car. Fortunately for their plan, the engine, wheels, and control center for the cable car lies at the top of the mountain so that no attendant remained outside the car to observe their skillful leap. A pity that, as it was a thing of beauty well worth noting.

The wind blows at them as they settle in. Kip looks up the cable line. Looks like a long ride. The cable car moves up the mountain with its passengers; the unsuspecting below and the unsheltered above. A beautiful mountain and a very long trip up. Had a look at the cable car run to the castle in *Where Eagles Dare* lately? Go look. We'll wait.

See. A long way.

Kip and Trevor hang on for dear life, wind whipping around them. No dashing about on this trip. They'd sue their travel agent if they had one. They grip the cable car with the audacity of cavemen, lips sea blue in the cold. Good thing they picked a summer date; this would prove impossible in winter.

As the cable car approaches the upper cable car room, Kip and Trevor leap off onto the canopy to the cable car building. They make their way to the window. There they can watch the arrival ceremony in concealment.

Upper cable car room – Abbey

A large mechanical room for the cable car equipment but also a sizable receiving area. The monks exit the car to find Count Orlok, dressed in General Staff gray, standing between mustered rows of his minions. These divide into brown-shirt functionaries, and lab-coated researchers. At the pride position of the later stands Doctor Damarung, shuffling his feet in irritation at needing to attend ceremonies. Karl, wearing Gestapo black with leather coat, now sporting arm band and insignia, stands next to General Orlok.

The monks array themselves before Orlok and his

reception committee. Kip and Trevor observe from the outside window of the cable car area. They can only see the backs of the monks, and hear next to nothing against the wind in their ears.

Count Orlok, "Brethren. Men of the Coming Times. Elect of ODESSA. I, your pastor and your leader, Keeper of our Holy Grail, director of our efforts toward the Final Resolution, I, Count Superior Field Marshal Frederick von Orlok, direct descendent of the great General Otis von Orlok of our Finer Days, bid you: welcome."

Murmurs. Orlok makes a grand gesture with his arms, "You may unveil."

They do.

Kip and Trevor watch from above as the robes come off.

Trevor, "Nazis!"

Kip, "Didn't see that coming."

The guests have removed their monk's robes, revealing themselves. Orlok notices an anomaly in his flock. Rafe offers a friendly wave. Orlok remains unflappable as ever.

Count Orlok, "If I may ask."

Dieter steps forward to make introductions, "Count Orlok, I have the honor of introducing descendent Archduke Ivan Dragomiloff Kopopkin and," he chokes with pride, "the last of the Romanovs: Anastasia the Fifth, Czarina of all the Russians!" Applause and hurrahs from the Abbey guests, all now proud of their new friends and their touch with greatness. Who knew what heights of status ODESSA had reached before this quinquennial?

Orlok nods to Rafe and Natasha, "I welcome you, honored guests."

Rafe clicks his heels.

We should, however, pause to note the puzzled expression of Rafe, a man now being honored and welcomed, who but a moment ago assumed he would be arrested and beaten. Nor does the absurdity escape Natasha. But Natasha gives no expression to her surprise, as befits a spy of the first rank, and a Czarina of all the Russians.

And although Orlok isn't about to ruin the moment, nor suggest to his guests and patrons that the leader of the Elect of ODESSA might have let interlopers into the inner sanctum of the order, nevertheless, he motions slightly to Karl to remain with a guard.

Count Orlok, "I dismiss the staff." Damarung and the rest of the staff depart. Orlok continues, "And now honored guests, let us tour the Abbey of the Eagles."

As sunset nears Orlok tour-guides while Rafe, Natasha and the brown-shirt ODESSA visitors listen attentively. Some take snapshots for their photo albums. Behind this group, Kip and Trevor sprint from one place of concealment to another, laden with backpacks, inappropriately dressed for a Nazi monastery. They run from shadow to shadow, in what they hope to be an inconspicuous manner, trying to both see and remain unseen.

Count Orlok, "Carthusian monks built the Abbey in 1879, and modifications have continued since then. Our order acquired it in 1945, after the unfortunate demise of the last of the Carthusians." Orlok lowers his head for a moment in commemoration of the last Carthusian. Orlok gives a well-rehearsed tour, you must say that for him. "The cable car upon which you arrived was built in 1925. Today it is our only entry, as we long ago blocked even the lower mountain passage used by the early Carthusians. Our Abbey could not be more secure."

Rafe and Natasha might take issue with that, but under the circumstances, best to let it pass.

Lower mountain side – nearing sunset

Marcy and Papa Cohen stand behind a row of small boulders, looking at something ahead of them. Marcy glances at Papa Cohen for a moment, then ahead again. Then Papa Cohen glances at Marcy for a moment, then ahead again. From their sheltered position they see a bit of a mountain side, perhaps where a rockslide once occurred. It explodes. As the dust settles, Marcy, Chris, and the Cohens approach the rubble of the rocks that had moments ago covered an opening to a mountain cave.

Abbey cloister – near sunset

The tour proceeds through the cloister. The cloister is a square courtyard enclosed by a square walkway itself covered by a roof. The courtyard has paths crisscrossing its grounds to the covered walkway. In the courtyard center lies a fountain. The square of the cloister, forming walls on the side of the covered walkway not adjoining to the courtyard, is composed of long rectangular buildings, some of them two stories and overlooking the cloister grounds. The side of the church forms one of the cloister walls. One may enter the cloister from any of its corners. A modest sized cloister overall, from one covered walkway to the other a person could throw a baseball and hit an opposite walker, but you would need to put a little arm into it.

Orlok leads the tour where monks once circled (or *squared* one presumes) in meditation, "Our cloister. Above, rooms for our special guests; those contributing at the Founders Level. Lovely rooms overlooking the cloister courtyard. I urge those still considering it to finalize your donations. Tonight, before the great banquet, our highest level of contributors will join me in the ceremony of initiation, commencing before our Greatest Relic, in our Inner-Most Sanctum." He pauses for affect, "Also, I will issue special robes and titles."

Rafe and Natasha look for opportunities to break away from the tour, but they notice that Karl and two large brown-shirt goons, all armed with classic luger pistols, keep them closely watched.

Count Orlok, "This way gentlemen. My lady."

The group exits the cloister to the northeast.

Kip and Trevor huddle against a cloister wall, watching them leave.

Kip, "I would describe our current position as dangerously conspicuous."

Trevor, "Owing to a grossly deficient briefing from headquarters, I neglected to pack my Hitler Youth uniform."

Kip, "Look."

Following Kip's finger, Trevor sees, at the opposite walkway, a lab coated technician leading a hairy-man on a chain. While obviously fully covered in hair, the hairy-man also presents a certain animal aspect beyond his furry figure. You might describe him as vaguely wolfish, although you would not feel justified in putting a pitchfork through him.

Kip, "We must be at the right place. Lab coats, hypertrichosiatic prisoners, and, uh, Nazis, of course. Somehow."

Trevor agrees, "At this abbey, somewhere, Marcy must be on the trail of Formula XOX. But how she blends in with this bunch escapes me entirely."

Kip points again to the lab technician and the hairy-man, "Well no one worries about those two. I'll bet he's taking that poor fellow to the lab."

Trevor, "And thus to the formula."

Kip, "And to Marcy too. We've practically solved this thing. We just follow them."

They do.

Outside the Abbey charter house – near sunset

The charter house: a round building outside the cloister, near the church, across from the exterior crypt entrance. All worked in granite. It sports small stone pseudo-buttresses all around, ornate and clearly to no engineering purpose, they sum up the charter house perfectly.

Count Orlok, "Behind us we have passed the exterior entrance to the crypts. Ahead of us, the old charter house."

As I said.

Count Orlok intones on entombment in his patented laconic manner, "I am honored to have my forefathers placed in the Abbey crypts. Their presence, entombed in our most sacred space, gives me great comfort. Take note that our Brotherhood extends this honor also to our highest elect. A special thanks we extend most willingly in light of their great contributions to our Order."

Rafe cannot help but admire the determined and unending sales pitch.

Count Orlok, "And before us now gentlemen," a nod to Natasha, "my lady. Before us, the old charter house." Orlok pauses gravely. Gravity does not exactly stand out on Orlok given his usual manner, but he puts a bit more grave into his standard weightiness now, "Once, the charter house hosted the meetings of the leaders of the Carthusians. Now it contains our Most Sacred Relic. Our Holy Grail. The hopes of all mankind. The very point and purpose of ODESSA. Awaiting a Suitable Vessel, and the day of the Final Resolution."

A moment of grave silence follows. Tears of awe fill sentimental Nazi eyes. Rafe, misreading the room, puts on a face of great sadness and woe. His lower lip quivers, the wrong sort of tear creeps into his eye.

Natasha jabs him in the ribs and shoots him a glare.

Orlok lets the moment last, then renews his pitch, "And here also will take place our special ceremony for our most elect. Anyone still considering investiture in ODESSA's highest honor may leave their contribution with myself, or Karl."

The tour moves on.

Outside the Abbey exterior crypt doors

The technician in the lab coat holding the manacled hairy-man opens the door to the crypt. It swings slowly on its hinges. Behind him, Kip and Trevor watch while trying to become one with the wall upon which their backs press. The technician in the lab coat and his charge disappear down the crypt, the door still open. Kip and Trevor follow.

Outside the Abbey library – near sunset

The tour continues. The tourists walk paths past the block masonry buildings. Cobblestones beneath and granite rising round, the Abbey feels like a sarcophagus awaiting the placement of its lid. A meditative mausoleum in the sunset, night promises to make it a sepulchral ensnarement. The tourists snap pictures.

Count Orlok, "The Abbey library and scriptorium. I have made it my private study. My own little sanctuary from the bustling world. Enclosed in stone, it contains whole worlds within."

Rafe wonders how much bustle the Abbey contains when not hosting ODESSA's quinquennial meeting. They must do *something* here in the off season.

Count Orlok, "It contains a collection of our movements most wonderous and serene art and the crafts which so define us. I have, conscientiously, added to that collection over the years. It is my great privilege to surround myself with the beauty ... of our most sacred order."

Inside at the dungeon stairs – near sunset

Yes dungeon. Even the Carthusians needed discipline. Maybe especially the Carthusians. Kip and Trevor descend the stone stairs barely lit by dim yellow lighting clearly added after initial construction. Ahead of them they hear low clanging and German cussing. No one cusses quite like a German; concentrated and guttural.

The stairs continue down, but the noises come from a passageway before them. Kip and Trevor peer into the passage to see the dungeon proper. Dark, cold, lithic walls, and lit, barely, by old lights drilled into the walls with thick cables carrying power. No one has bothered to make the dungeon pretty. That's just the way it is with dungeons. And what, one may ask, does an abbey dungeon contain? In this one at least: cages. And plenty of them. Hard to make out in the dim light, and unexpected in an abbey—even a Nazi abbey, one supposes—but nonetheless, cages.

In the cages Kip and Trevor see hairy-people. These seem mostly human, by no means fierce, but more like the animals they resemble. A hairy-man-chimp, a hairy-man-pig, several hairy-man-wolves or maybe man-dogs, and two hairy-monkey-children, among others. All in all, a lot of hair. And, more sinister, a clear leap back in human evolution while also simultaneously a leap forward in evil Nazi schemes. For a master race the Nazis have a real talent for knocking humanity back.

Trevor cringes, "Can't say I care much for this."

Kip, "Not a lab."

Trevor, "More like where they keep the specimens, I should say."

Kip, "Where did the guy go?"

Trevor, "Split up and look for him."

They enter the dungeon and take opposite routes around cages. The smell nearly overwhelms poor Trevor's delicate nose. His eyes, barely adjusted to the dark, now struggle against tears from the odor and the general shagginess of the place. In the poor lighting, a hairy-pig-man reaches out for Trevor, making Trevor jump—into a man wearing a lab coat.

Trevor, "I say! Terribly sorry!"

Lab technician, "Who are you?"

Trevor, "I'm on the tour, actually; seemed to have lost my guide."

The lab technician starts to point up the stairs when Kip knocks him out from behind.

Trevor, "What ho!"

Kip, "I am getting good at that."

Trevor looks at the unconscious lab technician with pity, "Looks so peaceful now, but later ... not to mention that I rather doubt he will answer any questions in that condition."

Kip, "We don't need him, just his clothes."

Trevor, "To go where precisely?"

Kip, "Obviously he came from the lab, so we go where he came from; find this Doctor Damarung; find Formula XOX; find Marcy; hop on a cable car roof, and *poof*. Mission accomplished."

Trevor, "All well and good, but we have only one disguise."

Kip Carson: a man never at a loss for a disguise, "Drop your pack." They both drop their packs. Kip rummages through his, pulling out his Lon Chaney disguise glue-set.

Trevor, "Hardly a time for your artistic endeavors."

Kip opens up Trevor's pack.

Trevor, "I say."

Kip pulls out Trevor's grooming and trimming set, "I can disguise you perfectly. What came here leaves here," he points to himself, "Lab guy," he points to Trevor, "Wolf-guy. God knows we have enough hair in here to work with."

Trevor loses it, "Wait one minute! I'll not become hirsute!"

Kip, "We only have one lab coat."

Trevor, "Be my guest! I'll stay behind and guard the menagerie!"

Kip, "We have to go together."

Trevor, "Then you go as *Wolf-guy*. I'll jerk your chain around the Abbey."

Kip, "I'd love to. Performance of a lifetime. But I'm the only one who knows how to make a creature effect, and I can't do it on myself."

Trevor offers a look of horror.

Inside a cave

Marcy, Chris, and the four Cohens, Papa, Hadassah, Ehud, and Ezra, ascend stairs cut into rock with only large flashlights to light their way. The stone stairs ascend from the lower caves. The stairs spiral their way up a giant cavern, often leaving an abyss just below their feet. Once, Carthusian monks made their way to the Abbey in meditative stages (resting for breath). This happened rarely, given their vows of isolation. Much more frequently, coolies hauled up food and supplies for the monks, with much cursing and fewer rest stops. The current commando team splits the difference; no curses, no rest. The stairs beneath them occasionally crumble underfoot.

Marcy, "How do you know about this place?"

Papa Cohen, "My great grandfather worked as a mason. He repaired these works. My grandfather sealed the entrance."

Chris shows great excitement, "I cannot believe this. I am storming a castle! I am actually storming a castle!"

Marcy, "An abbey."

Chris, "Still! Secret passages to a werewolf lair!"

Marcy, "I wouldn't count on werewolves."

Chris, "I can see why you love your job."

Marcy, "Typically I do more paperwork than this."

A bit of Grandpapa Cohen's stonework gives way beneath her, falling into the dark abyss.

Marcy, "Much more paperwork."

Inside the Abbey church – sunset

Orlok leads the tour through the church, centerpiece of the Abbey of the Eagles. The Carthusians built the church in granite, very traditional, not a cathedral in size by any means, but in that spirit. They adorned it with stain glass windows, of the first quality. Since their day, the Abbey's newest masters have added their own windows; second tier quality, not cheap, but the Vatican's Monsignor for Stain Glass Window Quality Control would send them back. Still, wholly functional, and at this moment they give a hint of outside light as the sunset fades into evening.

Count Orlok, "A lovely interior, late Gothic in design. Stonework done by local masons; the granite quarried locally. The stain glass comes from Germany. And here before us, our most recent window, courtesy of your kind donations." Orlok stops beneath a large stain glass window rising above them. It depicts Hitler in lederhosen receiving a wreath from, one presumes, heaven.

Rafe, disbelieving his eyes, "That's Hitler."

Natasha looks at Rafe as her infiltration and concealment instructor once looked at her on her first day of training—when she was eleven years old.

Orlok clears his throat, "Moving on."

They move on through the church. Natasha notes that in place of pews the church contains benches and tables, big blocky wooden affairs placed in rows down the naïve; more the look of a beer hall laid out for Oktoberfest than a church. All face an alter and podium, with chairs on either side of the speaker's platform. Men in brown-shirts put out beer steins and plates.

Count Orlok, "We prepare now, as you can see, for tonight's general celebration and the announcement of new honors. I will present our new Elect. I shall outline our five-year plan. We shall raise a—stein—for our Order. There will be much rejoicing."

They leave the church by its front entrance onto the Abbey grounds.

On the Abbey grounds – bell tower – evening

Orlok leads the tour out into the fresh evening air. He arranges them in front of the church's arched entry so that they may better observe its masonry. High relief carved figures adorn the stone arch, only a few of them re-carved into the likeness of a Heinrich Himmler or Hermann Goring. This to the relief of high relief carving enthusiasts, but to some dismay among the current clutch of tourists. Fear not, Orlok offers a solution, "We continue, most diligently, with the re-carving of the grand church entry. Ever making the Abbey of the Eagles our own. Even the stone we refashion in our likeness, that it may submit to our great mission. Your donations advance this effort enormously." Nods all around. Rafe himself affects the look of a man on the cusp of writing a check.

Orlok indicates a tall bell-tower to his right. It rises from the front of the church. Built in granite like the church, it rises high above it, ending in four long stone columns forming open air rectangles that reveal the bell within and support the pointed roof above.

Count Orlok, "Our bell-tower. The stairs lead to its high opening from which I invite you to enjoy the magnificent view of the valley below. I find it myself a place of great solace." Then the kicker: "We ring the bell every April 20th." Orlok gathers his sheep to move on, "Let us now proceed to the old infirmary."

Rafe does not understand why some of the brown-shirts chuckle at this.

Within the dungeon

A hairy-man squats in his cage with all his hair shaved off. This sounds like just a *man,* but it looks far more uncanny than that. The hairless hairy-man, none the happier for having his hair shorn, retains some aspect of a wolf. Still, you wouldn't call him a wolf-man, in no small part because it is hard to believe that a wolf-man would deign to suffer such an indignity. Furthermore, he shuffles about in his cage, disgruntled and meek. He possesses none of the aggression needed to hunt upon the moor and bay at the moon to terrorize the townsfolk. He misses some key ingredient. Besides, of course, his hair.

A few feet back from the cage, the unhappy recipient of this hair squirms under its application. Kip works to glue hair on a cringing Trevor. Trevor already sports the blue-collar shirt of the hairy-folk and has been covered in fleece. Kip works on the back of the neck—perfecting his wolf-man.

Kip, "Hold still."

Trevor, "Itches like the devil."

Kip, "That's the glue. I'm using a lot, so it doesn't come off."

What a relief.

Outside the Abbey laboratory – night

The laboratory; every abbey has one. Though less Gothic in design than the rest of the Abbey, and squatter, it still expresses a love of stone's unbreakable permanence.

Count Orlok, "Our laboratory."

The very idea of this shakes Rafe's tongue loose, "For religious experimentation? Buddhism? Re-mixing the trinity?"

Natasha could strangle him sometimes.

Count Orlok, "A jest. The laboratory, of course, serves as the locus for our experiments in search of a Suitable Vessel."

Rafe, "For the Final Resolution."

Count Orlok, "Exactly."

Rafe knows exactly nothing about what either of them mean, but he has gotten the hang of the local vernacular. It helps to pronounce everything like a title God Himself would hand out. Orlok leads the tour past the lab.

Within the Abbey novice quarters – ground floor – evening

A hallway, made of stone, punctuated with large old oak doors separating the cells. Not much to see. A disappointing end of tour one might think.

Count Orlok, "Once this building housed the novices. We have converted the cells above to hold," he smiles back at Rafe and Natasha, "uninvited intruders."

Gulp.

The tour proceeds down the hallway. Above, from the ceiling and so from a cell on the second floor, the tourists hear a pounding sound. Something stomping on the floor above; something big. Everyone looks up, but Orlok walks on, like a man made deaf by necessity.

At the end of the dormitory hallway Orlok stops and turns, "And here our tour comes to its conclusion, at our Abbey Gift Shop." He gestures at the gift shop. It looks like every other gift shop in the world, allowing for all the swastikas. "All major credit cards accepted." Renewed excitement grips the crowd; every tourist loves a gift shop. They pour into it. Rafe and Natasha try to follow, but Orlok raises a hand in objection.

Count Orlok, "I wonder if I could trouble the two of you to join me in my library. For a private drink."

Rafe, "Oh. I had hoped to find some Third Reich playing cards. Maybe a Hitler key chain. A mask for Halloween." Karl and the goons step forward, lugers drawn.

Rafe, "Maybe after."

Within the Abbey library – night

Orlok entertains Rafe and Natasha as they sit before the fireplace, *Adolf in Glory* looking down upon them, Nazi objects d'ugly all about them. Karl serves cognac while two goons stand by the door.

Rafe, "Love what you've done with the place."

Count Orlok, "Unfortunately, every five years I must convert my study into a setting suited to impress potential patrons at ODESSA's quinquennial meeting."

Rafe sips his cognac; looks like he had better tuck in for a long stay. Natasha studies Karl and the goons for weaknesses. Natasha, a study in strength, studies weakness.

Count Orlok, "The brethren have never been known for their aesthetic taste, and I fear we have suffered increased decadence over the generations. They have traded the arts of war for wars of trade. Once mighty in daring battle's fortunes, today they supervise concrete factories, administer payroll disbursements, perform due diligence reviews, coordinate event planning, inspect for regulation compliance, control expenditures, manage assets. I fear they *Don the Brown* only as a hobby. An affectation. An indulgence in nostalgia."

Rafe, "Why not kick the bounders out?"

Count Orlok, "I am heir to what one might call a family business, begun by my grandfather, one of the first members of the SS to realize that, tragically, the Fuhrer's vision could not become reality in his own lifetime. My grandfather slipped out of Germany and founded the order here, on safer ground."

Rafe, "What year was that?"

Count Orlok, "Nineteen forty-one. The man was a visionary."

Rafe will drink to that.

Count Orlok, "All this we owe to him." Orlok gestures grandly. He looks about, realizes the current state of decor, and shudders. "My father took up the reins of command and passed them on to me as my time arrived. I carry on the family tradition. The tradition of ODESSA." Orlok straitens in pride. His bearing, already so strait, can stand only marginally more straitening, but he straitens a bit all the same. "Perhaps our Brotherhood has itself suffered a decadent decline in the years since our founding. I admit that the running of the Order has slipped into routine, but I fill my own days with beauty." He gestures above the fireplace, then remembers. "Ordinarily."

In the guise of looking at the painting, Natasha checks the windows as a possible escape route.

Count Orlok, "But enough of me. I so long to hear *your* story. How do you come to be at my abbey Archduke Kopopkin?" Orlok pronounces the name as if he thinks it ridiculous, emphasizing the *pop*.

Rafe lives for this stuff, "Well, the Czarina and I are on tour, building support for a restoration of the monarchy— on strictly conservative lines of course—heard about your outfit and thought you might sign a petition; for the right donation, obviously, and maybe a wall plaque. Bronze I think. Embossed with: *ODESSA*." Rafe frames the imagined plaque with his hands.

Natasha doesn't think much of this story, but she tries to look regal.

Count Orlok, "History being one of my particular

avocations, I would be most fascinated to meet an actual descendent of a White Russian General. However, I can't say I've ever heard of a General *Kopopkin*. Much less an Archduke of that name."

Rafe, "An alias of course. My great grandfather's actual name was Ivan Dragomiloff Ivanov..." Rafe checks for recognition in the face of Orlok. Nothing.

" ... Demetriov ..."

Nope.

" ... Chugunev ..."

Nada.

" ... Agapor ... Degtyarev ... Kalashnikov ..."

Yikes! No.

" ... Ovechkin ..."

Natasha remains stoic.

" ... Talanov ... Savisin ... Perestoronin..."

Wait. Orlok smiles and nodes his head in recognition. So Rafe stops, and prays he never needs to repeat his over-grown pseudonym, or even remember the last name he offered.

Count Orlok, "Ah yes. The General Archduke Perestoronin. I recall him."

Rafe, "Dear old Great Granddad—I hasten to point out we all just called him *Ivan*." Rafe glances at Natasha, rather proud of himself. How's that for out Russianing the Russian Femme Fatale? Where would she be without him?

Natasha shakes her head at Rafe just slightly.

Count Orlok, "General Perestoronin, traitor to the White Russian cause. Later Bolshevik Commissar in the Caucasus as I remember from my readings."

Not good.

Rafe, "Bit of a black sheep, Uncle Ivan."

Orlok waves a dismissive hand, "All nonsense."

Correct.

Within the dungeon

Trevor looks the proper wolf-man. Covered in hair, face and hands and all; puffy with hair beneath his blue shirt and ragged at the bottom of his pants.

Trevor, "How do I look?"

Kip, "Stoop down some."

He does.

Kip, "Paw the air with your claw hands."

He does, reluctantly.

Kip, "Growl."

Trevor, "Don't be absurd, they don't growl."

Kip, "It would bring out the whole ensemble."

Trevor, "Put the bloody manacles on me."

Kip picks up the manacles. He puts the chain around Trevor's waste and puts Trevor's wrists into the manacles, snapping them shut. Kip instructs Trevor in the operation of the restraints.

Kip, "Here's the latch. In—out—over." The manacle opens. "Just difficult enough to foil an ordinary wolfman."

Trevor, "But not an English wolfman."

Kip smiles. "Not an English wolfman."

Within the Abbey library – night

Rafe carries on gamely, "Okay. The story. The real one this time. My colleague and I, we aren't Russian at all."

Natasha crooks her head at him as if to ask, *why*?

Rafe, "We belong to a humanitarian organization, dedicated to the brotherhood of mankind. We are the—" Rafe launches his organizational random name generator, "International Social Religious Altruistic Enterprises League. Or, as we call it—"

Natasha grinds her teeth while Rafe reviews his creation for the correct acronym.

He finds it.

Rafe, "Oh. Well, we just call it that." Rafe moves on, "Anyway, we're a humanitarian group. Altruists. And we have noticed, our organization I mean, we have noticed a real prejudice against Neo-Nazis."

Orlok cuts him off, "We are not *neo*. We are *classic*." Rafe looks amazed at the distinction, but clearly Orlok places some importance on it.

Rafe, "Even more so against classic Nazis. Have you noticed how little hesitation writers have about making fun of classic Nazis? Or making them the villains of the story? And just because you're hate-filled bigots with a history of extreme violence. Not that I'm judging, mind you." Rafe struggles, glances at Natasha. No help there. Why doesn't she ever kick in with anything? Rafe struggles on alone, "I'm sure you can't help yourselves. Who can help being hostile to ordinary standards of decency? What kind of responsibility could a person have for how they, uh, treat people?"

Orlok waits patiently.

Rafe, "I mean to say, in all sincerity, we came to help. Help explain you to the world. We want to make your case before the world. As humanitarians." Rafe smiles, hoping a smile will put all this over on the Nazi.

Count Orlok, "Further nonsense."

It seems nothing can stop ODESSA.

At the lower dungeon stairs

Marcy, Chris, and the Cohens ascend through the cave stairs to the lower Abbey stairs. Now they have not a looming abyss below, but proper rock walls on both sides. In the beams of their flashlights they see crosses carved into the walls.

Marcy, "Signs of habitation ahead."

Chris indicates the carved crosses, "These signs. They suggest we approach a crypt."

Marcy, "Semiology to the rescue."

Chris, "Still can't see anything but stairs ahead. Who knew international policing involved so much leg work."

Within the Abbey library

Rafe looks tired but defiant, "Okay, fine, we might as well have it out. I'm Rafe Riley, confidence trickster and Interpol agent. She's Natasha, also with Interpol. She's Russian, I'm not." Rafe recognizes that his ethnic identifications have lost a little credibility, but he presses on, "Interpol sent us to find Marcy Gainer, Interpol executive supervisor and mother of one." Rafe gives Orlok a hard stare, "I think you know who I mean."

Orlok does not appear to know who he means.

Rafe, "You kidnapped her."

Nothing.

Rafe, "You kidnapped her and took her out to sea."

Still nothing from Orlok, which is a pity because Rafe could really use some help here. Just as well Rafe does not look at Natasha right now, as her look of disbelief at his obtuseness would not inspire confidence.

Rafe, "We tracked her through her husband; his bulletin board." Rafe looks about. "You must have him around here too. I cracked the clues. K Attler. Mr. Cargo. Number 107. Minus 3. Interpol knows all about your completely evil cult now. You might as well give up, before our rescue team gets here." Rafe decides to stretch the bluff just one last little bit, "I think half of them are Jewish, and they aren't going to like all this one little bit."

Orlok nods.

Rafe glances at Natasha. Natasha rolls her eyes. Why does she never help?

Count Orlok, "Your most preposterous story yet. I can see we will get nowhere with these civilized methods. I had hoped that with some cognac and conversation we might avoid ugly necessities. But alas." Orlok shakes his head and purses his lips at the futility of kindness, "Tomorrow, when our guests have gone, we will begin a more, classic, approach. For now, I fear you will both need to occupy a cell in the Chamber of Novices."

Orlok almost gestures to Karl, but then Natasha rises,

"I am Natasha Raskalitkanof, Agent of ODESSA, the Organization of Former SS Officers. I work in Ukrainian Division under Klaus Fuchs. I have spent the last year infiltrating Interpol. The Idiot Man is Interpol agent, his only honest words. He came to infiltrate and sabotage Kloster Adler. I came to stop him."

Count Orlok looks intrigued. Rafe could not be more confused.

Count Orlok, "And I presume Herr Fuchs will vouch for you?"

Natasha, "Call him."

Count Orlok, "That requires a trip into town. But tomorrow."

Natasha, "Good."

Orlok smiles, a rather sinister smile, "One thing more."

Orlok puts his index finger against his chin, as if thinking. His middle finger and thumb he presses together, forming a bird-beak. He lifts his third finger up, with the pinky tucked beneath it.

Without a moment's hesitation Natasha flashes the counter sign: index finger on her temple, middle finger on her chin, third and pinkie pressed against thumb forming a downward looking bird-beak.

Orlok stands up, "Welcome Agent Raskalitkanof!" He shakes her hand. "I am most surprised. Gratified as well. I await your report. Of course, I will need to confine you for the night until we can confirm your identity with Herr Fuchs."

Natasha, "Of course."

Count Orlok, "But, in comfort." Orlok calls the goons, "Bruno. Would you and Gunter be so kind as to escort Agent Raskalitkanof to a suite over the cloister and," Orlok nods graciously toward Natasha, in apology, "Lock her in." Natasha clicks her heels, rather more convincingly than Rafe, and departs under guard.

Rafe looks back and forth between the two of them,

123

his jaw slack in classic mouth-breather array. Somehow, everything, absolutely everything on this mission has gotten past him. He tries to work backwards to find his mistake, starting with the last heel-click and moving meticulously all the way back to his childhood. But no, apart from that unfortunate two weeks dating Lucy Bevenhouse in tenth grade, nothing stands out as both erroneous and explanatory.

Orlok turns to Rafe, "And Karl will, I'm afraid, escort you to less comfortable lodgings."

Orlok smiles, sardonically. Karl smiles, sadistically. And Rafe? Rafe doesn't smile at all.

Within the church – crypt entrance

Kip and Trevor discover the crypt door into the church, opposite the door from the crypts to the exterior paths through which they had earlier entered. The crypts, thus, like death itself, bridge the sanctity of the holy ground and the profane world beyond. Or did when the Carthusians ran the place.

Kip holds Trevor's chain and motions him to hunch down animal-like. Trevor hunches, more like a man hunching than an animal, but given that he is a master cracksman and not a mime, not bad. As they walk into the church, approaching its center crossing, they see preparations for ... a party?

A big man in a brown shirt, yells at Kip, "Get that thing out of here!"

Kip gives a *who me?*

The man shouts, "Use the other crypt exit. Don't bring freaks through the beerhouse." So preserving a sacred space after all.

Kip and Trevor retreat from the "beerhouse" back through the crypt entrance.

Within a hallway above the cloister – guest quarters

Bruno opens the door; Gunter stands by, gun in hand.

The door swings open to reveal a very comfortable room, elegantly appointed in a manner entirely not in keeping with a monastery. A beautifully quilted Euro-sized comforter covers a four-post bed which faces a Devon and chair separated by an enormous five-foot solid iron candle-holder. The windows have thick curtains worked by thick curtain ropes. A baroque eyeful meant, no doubt, to impress the master-race tourist.

Bruno motions Natasha in with a grin more evil than kind. She enters. Bruno shuts and locks the door. He and Gunter walk down the hallway, smiling that they once again find themselves on the better side of a locked door. Agent or not, they have the woman hopelessly trapped. Good days work for a classic Nazi. They leave the hall.

Silence. Dust drifts down to settle on the wooden floor of the hall.

A massive impact shatters the door of Natasha's quarters, turning into splinters. The hammer: A giant iron candle-holder suspended from curtain ropes. Natasha drops her home-made swinging battering-ram. She steps through the splintered door. She no longer wears her dress, but only her black body-suit.

Natasha is done fooling around.

Within the lower crypts

Marcy, Chris, and the Cohens explore the lower crypts. Small vaults, cut into the rock, hold the bones of long departed brothers. More important brothers have stone tablets covering their ossuaries, telling in brief words the identity of the occupant and his hopes for the hereafter. The uninvited guests explore the tombstones with their flashlights, the only light in the crypt.

Chris, "The dates go back to 1880. Carthusian, I think." He reads a tombstone, "Alphonse Rodriguez. Beloved Prior, given to God in hopes of the Resurrection. June 9, 1885."

Marcy, "You read Latin?"

Chris, "Crypt Latin." He reads another, "Armand De Rico. Pious herbalist. Given to God March 17, 1892."

Marcy, "I feel a little uncomfortable about this. Like a grave robber."

Chris, "Welcome to my world. My other world. Not so many gun-fights but still plenty to feel guilty about."

Ahead of them Hadassah calls, "Chris. Come."

Chris, "What have you found?"

Hadassah, "Different stones."

Chris makes his way to Hadassah by the beam of his flashlight. Marcy follows.

On the Abbey grounds

Kip and Trevor walk the grounds. Night at the Abbey brings darkness, but occasional electric lights attached to various buildings provides some irregular illumination, as does light from windows. And naturally, they walk beneath a full moon, apropos to a werewolf story. Still, not easy to see.

Kip, "I can't see a thing."

Not at all easy to see.

Trevor, "Look for a lab."

Kip, "I can't see anything, and I don't know what a monastic laboratory looks like."

Kip sees a man in a lab coat pass under a light, "On the other hand." Kip and Wolf-man Trevor follow the lab coat man.

Within a hallway – Abbey novice quarters

An unhappy return for Rafe to the novice quarters. Did the Carthusian novices find it so grimly gothic? Does one better meditate on silence draped in stone? Rafe can't remember if the Carthusians took vows of silence. The only thing Rafe knows less about than monks is keeping silent. Rafe walks just ahead of Karl who keeps a hand on his holstered sidearm.

Karl, "I will very much enjoy tomorrow. I have a special

talent for making people talk."

Rafe, "Lucky day, I have a great talent for talking."

Dieter and Johan approach them coming from the opposite direction. Beer and giftshop bric-a-brac have put them in a fine mood. They smile at Rafe.

Dieter, "Archduke Kopopkin, what goes on?"

Rafe jerks a thumb back at Karl, "This traitor has captured me. Get him!"

Instantly Dieter and Johan attack Karl.

Karl, "No!"

Down goes Karl, the two thugs pounding away on him. Nothing like a good abbey brawl to put the best punctuation on a quinquennial meeting.

Dieter, still madly punching Karl, "Who is he?"

Rafe fast-walks away saying only, "Mossad."

They pound all the harder.

Rafe, "Have at him boys." Rafe escapes.

Out on the Abbey grounds

A brown-shirt worker stands beside a wall in the dark. He looks furtively around. Seeing no one, he takes out a cigarette and lights up. Apparently Orlok enforces a strict no smoking policy. Mr. Brown-Shirt takes one long drag from the cigarette. He looks up at the night sky. The majestic Milky Way. So many stars. They shine, pinpoints of light suspended in the ink dark. What would it be like to visit one? THUD. Something falls upon him from above, knocking him on to the ground and out cold.

Natasha picks up the cigarette and flicks it away. She takes a pistol from the brown-shirt man's holster. She moves on.

Within the church

Rafe walks into the church, rich with symbols, thick with Nazis. Stain-glass saints offering the Trinitarian Blessing rise beside midbudget stain-glass Famous Nazis of Yesteryear shaking their glassy iron fists. An apsidal chapel to the left invites prayers to St. Bruno of Cologne, while the apsidal chapel to the right bids the supplicant meditate on the bust of Martin Bormann. Beer replaces holy water in the stoup. The tabernacle transformed into a pretzel box (you can guess the shape of the pretzels). The Lectionary exchanged for *The Nuremburg Laws*. The chalice tossed out for a beer stein. Thugs with the thurible, rowdies at the reliquary, Nazis in the naves. All under a quadripartite vault.

Rafe notices brown-shirt table setters everywhere and makes a quick lunge to the first room he sees.

Within the vestry

An unfortunate choice. Rafe stands at the entry of the vestry looking at five burley Nazis in various stages of putting on ornate hooded robes. They stare at him for a moment. One recognizes him, "Archduke Kopopkin! You are joining the Elect of ODESSA?"

Rafe never misses a beat—his genius and his curse. "Why yes I am." Rafe takes up a robe to put on. No actual Carthusian ever wore this black and red, gold trimmed, swastika adorned, fur lined monstrosity to the eyes. Rafe doesn't care for the design, but he hasn't had a lot of wardrobe choices lately.

At least everyone in the room has a glad hand for the Archduke. Better than drawn lugers.

Within the Abbey library

Orlok wears elaborate robes, slightly reminiscent of the priestly robes of ancient Israel (cultural appropriation doesn't even count as venal sin to a Nazi). Orlok rehearses his investiture gestures as Doctor Damarung speaks his mind.

Doctor Damarung, "You have promised to make the great announcement tonight at the banquet."

Count Orlok, "My dear Herr Doctor, we have so much more research to do, years of research ahead of us." Orlok practices graceful movements in his robes. Pointing at this, indicating that. A hand raised in modesty; arms moved wide in welcome.

Doctor Damarung, "No! What more do we need to research? We have the formula in the cell. We have only to select a subject and the Blood of the Beast will do the rest!"

Count Orlok, "But what subject? Where could we find a suitable vessel?"

Doctor Damarung, "The Blood of the Beast will make the vessel suitable."

Count Orlok, "A theory Herr Doctor, only a theory."

The door flies open. Enter Karl, disheveled; black eye, bloody nose, fat lip (well, even fatter lip). He says, "Herr Count, the prisoner has escaped!"

Count Orlok, "Karl, your uniform! What's that? How did he escape?"

An embarrassing question, and surprisingly hard to answer succinctly. Karl says, "He overpowered me!" Moving on. "I am ready to sound a general alarm."

Orlok looks slightly alarmed at the idea of a general alarm, "No. No. We mustn't cause a scene. Not at this critical moment in our ... rituals. The man Rafe, or whomever he now purports to be, has nowhere to go. Post a guard on the cable car and let the matter rest for the moment. We will scour the Abbey tomorrow when our work is done, our ceremonies concluded, our funding secured, and our guests departed."

Doctor Damarung, "Herr Count. I do not mean to accuse you of treason to our cause."

Count Orlok, "Treason?"

Karl looks shocked as well; beaten up, and shocked.

Doctor Damarung, "But I will not stand for further delay."

Orlok takes on a reassuring tone, "Do not worry Herr Doctor, you will be most satisfied with the night's conclusion. I will address all of your concerns." Orlok practices a concern-addressing lift of his forefinger.

Doctor Damarung, "You will announce the Advent of our

Glory? You will tell the men of ODESSA this very night?"

Count Orlok, "Fear nothing."

The expression on the face of Doctor Damarung could not be described as reassured rather than, say, furiously skeptical.

Outside the Abbey laboratory

Kip and Trevor watch from a distance, hidden by darkness as the lab assistant they have followed enters the lab through its dimly lit door.

Trevor, "That must be the laboratory. In which we will find the object of our quest. The nefarious Doctor Damarung and the mysterious Formula XOX."

Kip, "And perhaps the fair maiden Marcy Gainer as well."

Trevor, "I frankly begin to suspect that Marcy inhabits this abbey as an entirely epistolary phenomenon. After all, how much credibility do we afford to an elderly babysitter moonlighting as a postal worker? Especially if we must imagine Marcy accompanied by a father and children. Did they leap upon the cable cars? Did they surmount the walls? Did they hide in the Abbey nooks and creep around its corners? Surely they received no invitations."

Kip, "I bet she came to rescue Chris. Why else would Marcy leave Katrina with a stranger?"

Trevor, "Chris? Kidnapped by Nazis?"

Kip, "Anything could have happened. Look at you right now, a werewolf. I'm just glad we didn't find them in the cages. Scares me to think of Chris and Marcy helpless in that dungeon."

Trevor, "Be that as it may. I feel certain of one thing at least: in a moment we shall enter the lab and render speculation superfluous. Let us proceed."

They approach the door and upon arriving face an unexpected practical problem of clandestine assault etiquette.

Kip, "Should we knock?"

Before they can puzzle out this question, something falls on them from above like a pouncing jungle cat—that knows karate—knocking Trevor out cold. A roundhouse kick flattens Kip.

Natasha stands alone.

Before she can inspect her dispatched targets, Natasha hears the shouts of approaching men. She takes off, a panther in the night.

Still boozed up and bloody knuckled, Dieter and Johan approach.

Dieter, "Who's there?" Dieter sees Kip, wearing a lab coat, and Trevor, fully furred, on the ground. Kip has survived the assault from above still sensate, but not yet understanding how the moon fell on him. He shakes his head, trying to clear it of the bits of brain now detached within and rattling about.

The two goons survey the scene before them and draw the obvious conclusion. Dieter grabs Kip and pulls him up, "Good job! Beast almost got away from you, but you took him out. Not bad for a scientist!"

Kip, "Huh?"

Kip's articulate response, so ripe with modesty, confirms his heroism to Dieter. Dieter gives Kip a hard slap on the back —Dieter's principal gift to the world and all therein—and congratulates him all the more, "I'll stand you to a drink at the banquet. Johan can take the beast back to the dungeon."

Kip, now suffering a spinal dislocation to accompany his concussion, looks confused, but what can he do in the face of such fellowship?

Outside of the Abbey charter house

Six men in elaborate robes stand in the dark before the charter house. Their hoods entirely conceal their faces, except when one or another peaks out from his monkly bonnet to have a better look. Rafe does this, then tucks back in as Count Orlok exits the charter house. Rafe notes, through the folds of his cowl, that Orlok now wears a ceremonial get-up that might be described as Ancient Hebrew Priest With Swastika Fetish.

Orlok stands before the six hooded men and gives his well-rehearsed speech, deploying his much-practiced gestures. "Welcome Elect of ODESSA. You who have served so well, sacrificed so willingly, contributed so much. Tonight, the night of your investiture, you will bear witness to our Highest Mystery, our most Sacred Relic, our Holy Grail, the beating heart of our Brotherhood. I invite you into our inner sanctum, our Holy of Holies."

With that, and the odd grand gesture or two, Orlok enters the charter house. The others follow, lifting up their ceremonial robes so as not to trip. An oddly dainty sight, all things considered.

Within the Abbey charter house

Inside: a single round room, the door through which they enter on one side, opposite it stands an altar. Immediately before the alter, and slightly below, lies a book-rest upon which rests a single open book. To the left of this stands an easel with a painting, to the right a poster sized photograph. All these face the alter and thus away from the Elect as they enter.

The rest of the room can best be described as Nazi Paraphernalia Explosion. Giant furled red swastika flags on poles cross above the door; others, elaborately unfolded, adorn the walls throughout. Some flags are gathered in gold braid at their base; others are gathered twice with gold and silver braids. Behind the alter two great monstrous red Nazi flags have been gathered and braided and tied together. Altogether, someone has put in a great deal of flag-furling time.

The well-furled flags frame paintings, themselves framed in swastika laden frames of gold and silver. The swastikas on the frames, carved into wood or impressed upon the metal, display great sumptuous patterns of broken crosses and mangled spider legs. Nazi enthusiasts have had a lot of time to doodle variations on the old favorite. What of the paintings themselves, so lovingly framed? Ordinary really. The stuff of old-time postcards. Buildings and landscapes whose technical competence cannot disguise their bleak monotony. They look dreary and conventional rather than intriguingly awful.

On pedestals throughout the room sit statuary suitable to the theme of the room. A bust of Hitler here, an eagle gripping a swastika there, and lots of Nordic men with big chests, posing as if for a gay men's magazine circa 1950. On an old television set against the wall, a recording of *Triumph of the Will* plays, sound turned down. Everything in the room leads the eye to the alter opposite the door. And on top of the alter? A covered object, not quite twice as tall as a life-sized bust, cylindrical in shape.

Orlok gestures so as to arrange his six inductees as a semicircle around the alter and the book-rest. Orlok himself stands next to the object of veneration, clearly planning an unveiling. How these Nazis love their unveilings.

Count Orlok, "From the ashes of defeat our brave forefathers of ODESSA brought this most sacred item, preserved as a living vessel by the wonder of Aryan science, to this Abbey of the Eagles. They bore every hardship, suffered every delay, endured every adversity. Every deed a testament to their courage and relentless determination. This Sacred Relic rests here not merely as an object of veneration, but as an authentic hope for our future, and that of all mankind."

Rafe's hood twitches back and forth as he tries to gage the reaction of his fellow Elect, but they all remain motionless in reverent anticipation.

Count Orlok, "Here the Sacred Relic awaits the creation of a Suitable Vessel, the aim of all our efforts, and of your contributions. We live for that day when such a vessel can be made, and it may walk again before us." Orlok reaches for a crescendo, "Here, I give you gentlemen, our illustrious past. Our glorious future. The answer to mankind's prayers."

This had better be good.

Count Orlok, "Gentlemen. I give you." Orlok lifts the veil, "Our Fuhrer!"

Unveiled: A vat filled with transparent fluid. And inside the vat, in the fluid: a brain. Complete with eyes.

Yes. *They Saved Hitler's Brain.*

"Heil Hitlers" ring out with accompanying salutes all around. Rafe's are a bit late and a little weak, but Orlok fails to notice as he himself hails Hitler's brain.

With the momentous unveiling done and the salutes over, Orlok returns to tour guide mode. "Rest assured gentlemen, our Fuhrer exists entirely sentient. His eyes see, his 'ears' hear. Those lines proceeding from the housing to the brain relay sounds from the audio receivers at the base of the vat to the appropriate cerebral structure." Orlok points in case we failed to notice the audio receivers at the base of the vat, being, as we were, so shocked at finding a brain inside of it.

Count Orlok, "The brain itself swells slightly when excited, as you see that it does now." We must take Orlok's word on this. "Although without eyelids of course, the balls of the eyes move to objects of interest." And in fact, the eyeballs do look about even as the eyes remain stationary.

Orlok strokes the case, "We try to make it comfortable. In this room," He gestures grandly. You can tell that Orlok most enjoys this part of his speech, "With objects of reassurance suggesting pleasant memories. His own paintings around him," Orlok's hand indicates the paintings around the room, ending with the painting atop the easel. It depicts the Vienna State Opera House as portrayed by a man who loves only Wagner. (The old cape trick indeed.) "Photographs," again Orlok gestures around the room, ending with the second easel holding a large picture of Hitler standing with Rudolf Hess in better days, "and on the lectern before his tank, his own favorite book: *Mein Kampf*. His struggle in print."

Rafe's hood twitches back and forth to gage reaction, and to ward off insanity. No one else gives any sign that either they, the world, or Rafe, has gone insane.

Count Orlok, "Each day, I, myself, turn the pages. On his birthday I display a novel. A Karl May western perhaps. It pleases him so." Orlok turns a page in demonstration. Elegantly done.

Count Orlok, "And of course, it watches television."

Within the upper crypts

Chris examines a tombstone, embedded in a wall, illuminated by the beam of a flashlight. Festooned in stone leaves, clutched by an eagle holding a swastika in its beak, it reads: *General Baron Alaric Frederick Orlok. August 17, 1928 – April 11, 1989. Bewahrer des Heilgen Relikts.*

Chris reads it aloud, "General Baron Alaric Frederick Orlok. August 17, 1928, to April 11, 1989. Preserver of the Sacred Relic."

Marcy, "Not a monk."

Chris reads the next one, "Colonel Otis Orlok, June 21, 1895, to February 25, 1968. Rescuer of the Sacred Relic."

Marcy, "Plus a Nazi."

Chris, "Yes. We seem to have found the Nazi section of the Abbey crypt."

Marcy, "And every abbey has one? I'm surprised at how normal you seem to find all this."

Chris, "I've toured the local gift shop. Not to mention the fact that I've been entertaining the possibility of werewolves for several days, so Nazi headstones in an abbey crypt carries only light shock for me at this point."

Hadassah calls from further inside the crypt, "Chris."

They enter another chamber of the crypt; their flashlight beams scour the walls. Swastikas everywhere. Not normal ones, but elaborate variations. Cross-bars through main-bars, third-bends to the ends, circles in the center. Like

Christian crosses elaborated by extra crosses, these spiders have evolved into baroque swastika wall art.

Marcy, "Someone got creative."

Chris, "Isolational variation. It happens when a subculture becomes symbolically inbred."

Marcy, "They got bored."

Hadassah, "They are Nazis." Her tone does not suggest someone taking notes on cultural anthropological theory. Her tone suggests, rather, someone about to deliver a world-of-hurt.

Marcy and Chris both know they tread on dangerous ground here. Marcy says, "We don't know that about the whole abbey."

Hadassah, "They are Nazis." Hadassah has some definite ideas about what one does when faced with a Nazi infestation.

Papa Cohen intervenes, "Hadassah. Patience."

A flashlight beam shines in from the other side of the chamber. Ehud steps in behind that light, "We have found more stairs. Going up. We see lights."

Hadassah turns and heads to Ehud. The others follow.

Within the dungeon

Johan carries an unconscious hairy-Trevor through the maze of cages to one near the far dungeon wall. The cage holds a hairy-pig-man who squeezes to the back as Johan opens the cage door. Johan dumps Trevor in and shuts the door. The hairy-pig-man looks at the hair covered and unconscious Trevor. The hairy-pig man stares at Trevor in something close to terror. Johan takes out a flask and, offering a toast to the room, has a bit of schnapps.

He leaves the way he came in, up the stairs. He walks up the stairs, out of sight, sipping schnapps. For a moment silence prevails in the dim light of the stairs. Then Ehud enters the dungeon, followed by Hadassah.

Away from this, in the far cage, Trevor opens his eyes.

Before him he sees the face of a hairy-pig-man. Trevor naturally assumes he has been condemned to hell. In a shaking voice he addresses the hairy-pig-man, "If *you've* come to guide me to the afterlife, I very much doubt I've made the cut." The hairy-pig-man retreats in fear. Trevor sits up and looks around. He sees damp gray walls and smells an uncleaned zoo odor. Not exactly hell, but not a place of reward either.

At the other side of the chamber, Ezra, Marcy, Chris, and Papa join Ehud and Hadassah at the dungeon entrance. They marvel at what they behold. A cavernous space full of cages filled with hairy-people.

Hadassah, "Wolfen."

Technically not correct, but you see her point.

Chris, "Nailed it!" Chris stands tall in triumph, "Ten points for anthropology!" He turns to Ehud, "Do you see this? I called it! They say I'll never finish my dissertation, but you put me in the field, two days tops, I find the werewolves. Take that ethnographic folklorists!"

Marcy, "Okay Chris."

Chris, "This Interpol stuff is so easy. Two months and I'll be running the organization."

Marcy, "Upper management uses a different skill set. Let's split up and search the room."

They enter taking different routes through the maze of cages.

At the dungeon's far end, Trevor opens his cage and steps out. He scratches his considerable chest hair. He walks tentatively through the cage maze. The hairy-people seem increasingly disturbed. They make animal noises. They grow louder. Trevor, not exactly in his comfort zone, grows nervous.

Marcy walks alone amidst the cages as the hairy-people grow more restless and shrill. Marcy doesn't know whether to fear or pity the beasts; especially the one that seems to have been ... shaved? Does someone breed these poor creatures for their hair? To make wigs? For nuns? Questions keep piling up and no sound theory unrelated to anthropology seems to help. Better just to carry on than to think too much at this stage. Marcy looks ahead of her at a slight opening among the cages illuminated by a light overhead.

Into the light steps: a wolfman!

A wolfman has escaped! Marcy freezes. The wolfman squints its eyes at Marcy, perhaps in preparation for an attack. Behind the wolfman Marcy sees Hadassah about to club the beast. The wolfman drops its squint.

Trevor, "I say, Marcy?"

Hadassah strikes! Down goes the beast. Chris runs forward from within the dungeon and sees the downed man-beast.

Chris, "Damn. That was close."

Silence.

Marcy, "Did it call me *Marcy*?"

Yes, Marcy, it did.

Within the Abbey church

A church, yes, strictly speaking, but currently outfitted as a beerhall. The brown-shirt men of ODESSA swill beer as if in some pseudo-Catholic Oktoberfest nightmare. All the drinkers sit on benches facing in the direction of the pulpit, at which Count Orlok stands. Flanking the pulpit, sit men in elaborate robes, three on each side, the new Elect of ODESSA.

We join Orlok in mid speech, "An Assemblage of Eagles as the world has never known." He offers his outstretched hands to the beer-swillers. The Eagles cheer themselves.

Count Orlok, "Men of Iron!"

In the front row of the men of iron, facing the pulpit, unadorned with a beer tankard, Doctor Damarung sits on the very edge of his bench in high expectation. He leans forward staring at Orlok, willing the Count's words onward. Damarung would make a puppet of Orlok if he could. His nervous energy could power his experiments right now. No one else in the spirited beerhall appears to take the proceedings so seriously. They drink and elbow each other in comradely, rib-bruising fellowship. Just good times for the classic Nazi.

Except in a middle row, next to a pair of burly beer-belchers (Dieter and Johan), where Kip sits, still garbed as a lab tech, and looking less like a man having a good time and more like one having just a little trouble determining what planet he resides on. Abbey's have churches, so good to go there. Nazis drink beer, one always took that for granted, so no worries there. The Nazis are drinking their beer in a church, with scientists, in front of—monks? Nazi monks. Kip cannot help but think that he has himself become a work of surrealist art. He has become the canvass indeed.

Within the dungeon

Trevor comes around. Chris kneels behind him propping him into the sitting position. Marcy kneels before him trying to coax the wolfman into speech. The Cohens watch.

Marcy, "Say *Marcy*. Can you say *Marcy*?"

Trevor, "Marcy?"

Marcy exults in this cross-species linguistic achievement, "It talks!" She turns her attention back to the wolfman, seeking to pry more amazing results from it, "Can you say anything else? Do you have a generalized power of speech?"

Trevor, "What?"

Marcy looks amazed, "If someone created this thing from a pure animal form, we're looking at a major scientific breakthrough."

Trevor, "What?"

Marcy points to herself for the benefit of the wolfman, "Me Marcy."

Trevor, "I bloody well know you're Marcy! What I cannot fathom, try though I might, is why everyone in this cursed place feels the uncontrollable urge to strike me upon the head. Blow upon dreadful blow. I could well understand if I were an unpleasant sort of chap, or even thought to be so, but no one even knows me here."

Marcy looks stunned, "Trevor? Is that you Trevor?"

Trevor, "Yes. Of course, it's me. Somewhere amidst the stars that twinkle now constantly before my eyes." Trevor tries to wave the stars away.

Marcy's eyes fill with tears, "Oh, Trevor. What have they done to you?"

Chris, too, can hardly believe the tragedy, "Is it the moon? Does the moon set you off?" Chris looks at Papa Cohen, "We have a full moon tonight." Chris looks to Trevor, "Does the moon transform you?"

Trevor grows irritated remembering who transformed him, "It was Kip Carson that transformed me if you really want to know!"

Tears roll down Marcy's cheeks, "Kip's a werewolf too? My God." Chris looks at Marcy hoping to comfort her with his eyes.

Trevor, "Whatever are you talking about? Kip has become a werewolf? Where? How?"

This confuses Marcy a bit, "Kip bit you?"

Trevor, "Kip bit me? Where?" Trevor starts looking for a bite wound.

Marcy, "You said Kip transformed you into a werewolf."

Trevor, "Have you gone mad? I'm not a werewolf."

Chris looks at Hadassah, "Denial. A normal psychological reaction to lycanthropic conversion."

Trevor looks behind him at who props him up, "Chris?" Trevor looks around, "Who are all these people?"

Marcy, "We will get you help. The best medical attention."

Trevor simply cannot process all this. He puts his hand on his aching head. He feels the fur-hair on his face and sees it covering his hand.

Trevor, "Oh."

Within the Abbey church

Orlok gives the impression of a man finally coming to the high point of his speech. Certainly the assembly pays rapt attention, between swallows. "So once every five years we gather to name and honor our most elite members. These men who have contributed so much to our beloved ODESSA."

The crowd grows excited, another unveiling!

Count Orlok, "Selected with the greatest care, invested with the highest authority, displaying the uppermost loyalty. They are the future of our great cause. With great pride, I give you the newest members of the Elect of our organization. The Men of Steel who lead the Men of Iron. The Eagles in our midst." He looks to the three robed men seated to his left, then to the three seated to his right, sucking every moment for drama. He looks to the audience as he gestures to the men seated on each side of him with wide open arms, "You may unveil!"

And the six men do. Applause all around. Orlok acknowledges the applause. He offers a gesture of honor to each man to his left, from the man who sits nearest to the man on the end. Each gesture brings more applause. Orlok likes to make this part special for the funders. He turns and does the same for the men seated to his right. Ending with Rafe.

Orlok does a double take. He looks for a moment at his lectern, as if this manifestation of his quarry might be explained in his notes. His notes do not help. He looks again at Rafe as the applause dies down.

Rafe nods to him. Good to be on board. Happy to serve.

Orlok closes and opens his eyes. Nope. Still there. Orlok notices that the applause has died down and that his audience waits to hear what's next. He sees Doctor Damarung about to fall out of his seat in anticipation. Unflappable as ever, Orlok pushes on. "Under my leadership, with the help of these men." He stumbles just slightly here before returning to his prepared remarks, "ODESSA has achieved many things."

Orlok carries on with the achievement list. No one notices anything amiss. But there is one person in the assembly even more taken aback than was Orlok to see Rafe unveiling himself with the honored guests. Kip squints at Rafe. He closes and opens his eyes. He looks down at the table before which he sits, as if rebooting, then looks up again. Rafe remains, smiling and oblivious to Kip in the crowd of ODESSA beer revelers. What does the mind create again? Kip needs help with this. He turns to drunken Dieter, "Say Dieter, how many people do you see on either side of the speaker?"

Dieter squints, "Twelve."

Not much help there.

Within the dungeon

Trevor stands now, a bit unsteady but under his own power.

Chris speaks to him in a gentle voice, "So why do you feel the need to look like a werewolf?"

Trevor sounds incredulous as he answers, "To walk the Abbey incognito, of course."

Of course.

Marcy needs to get her bearings, "You mean to say Kip is somewhere in the Abbey?"

Trevor, "Precisely."

Marcy, "But what are you doing here?"

Trevor, "I'm with Kip. Not at the moment manifestly, but in general. We are partners."

Marcy, "But what are the two of you doing at the Abbey?"

Now Trevor can get down to some serious briefing, "Like you, we follow the trail of the Secret Formula XOX. Like you, we have deduced that one Doctor Damarung invented this deadly serum. Like you, we rode the cable car roof to find our way here in search of the evil Doctor Damarung and his formula; surmising that we would find *both* here in this

Abbey of the Eagles—although the Formula XOX now exists only in a form no longer capable of being written down." Trevor pauses to consider this part, "Mind you, haven't figured that last bit out yet. Nonetheless, like you, we are on the case of the Secret Formula XOX. And like you, making considerable progress." Trevor seems pleased that at last he has made everything clear.

Marcy, "I've never heard of XOX. I'm on vacation."

Chris, "A working vacation. I do all the work. For both our jobs. I also do all the childcare."

Marcy, "Who is Doctor Damarung?"

Chris, "Did you say you rode on top of a cable car? Haired-up or before?"

The Cohen's appear interested in the talking were-beast who is only a hair-*loving* man and not legitimately hairy, but they also look impatient to get on with things.

Trevor, "I must say..." But he doesn't know what to say.

Chris, "Can I go back to something?" Chris shoots an apologetic look to the Cohens, "Sorry, but I still don't understand why Kip made you up to look like a werewolf."

Trevor, impatiently, "So that we might move through the Abbey inconspicuously!"

Marcy, "You mean to say that the Abbey is full of werewolves?"

Trevor leans in, finally able to impart something that is, comparatively, sensible, "No." The hammer drops, "The Abbey is full of Nazis!"

The Cohen's stiffen for a moment, then begin unloading their packs.

Marcy, "Nazis."

Trevor, "Nazis. All of them. Everywhere."

Chris throws up his hands, "Well, that did it. We're all done here folks."

Marcy looks around at the Cohens. Papa loads his machine gun with a belt of large caliber rounds. Ehud and Ezra sling submachine guns around their shoulders and put ammunition clips in their pockets. Hadassah straps on a dual holster with two gigantic .45 caliber semiautomatic pistols, one on each hip.

Marcy, "Wait. Should we talk first?"

Ehud and Ezra empty most of the rolls of dynamite from Hadassah's pack into satchels. Papa Cohen checks the workings of a radio detonator. Hadassah puts on her pack, empty now but for her own share of explosives. Ehud and Ezra sling the satchels of dynamite over their shoulders.

Marcy, "Stop." The Cohens pause and look at her. Marcy asks, "Why do you want to do this?"

Silence.

Marcy, "Okay. I see your point."

They return to preparing for Assault on Nazi Abbey.

Marcy, "But listen." Papa Cohen pauses. Marcy presses what case she has, "We have a man in there. An Interpol agent. One of us." Marcy gestures so as to include all of them, Cohen's as well. The Cohens listen. Marcy proposes a plan, "Let me take Trevor and move through the Abbey, incognito. We look for Kip while you plant explosives." She grabs a walkie-talkie, "When we find Kip, I'll give the word. You give us fifteen minutes to clear to the crypt entrance. Then bring the place down."

Papa Cohen looks at his kinder, "Yes. We will do this."

Chris nods vigorously in approval, "Great. Which team am I on?"

Marcy clips the walkie-talkie onto her waist. She turns to Chris, serious in tone, "You are on Team Katrina. We go up, you go down. And out."

Chris, "But I should be part—"

She cuts him off, "We each have our job to do."

Chris knows that a man must do what a man must do. And he has a child to care for. So he plays on Team Katrina.

Within the Abbey church

Doctor Damarung clutches the seat of his chair. The

ceremony has nearly ended, and he has heard no great announcement. He looks like a man putting his face in order in preparation for a nervous breakdown.

Orlok wraps things up, "Our glorious past leads us to a glorious future. Our struggles lead us to new struggles. Our memories of fallen comrades urges us to fight on." Tears fill the eyes of ODESSA men. Rafe tries to fake a few of these.

Count Orlok, "However long this struggle may last, however long it may take, however many more years we must fight on, we shall do so knowing that, someday, our efforts will herald in ... the *Final Resolution!*" Cheers all around. Heartfelt applause. Then the banquet breaks up. Good meeting. Inspirational.

Doctor Damarung looks near the breaking point, but Orlok pays him no mind. Instead, Orlok glances at two guards, Bruno and Gunter. They follow his eye to Rafe. Orlok gestures for his honored guests to follow him to the vestry. Orlok leads. The Elect follow. Bruno and Gunter fall in behind Rafe, hands on lugers, to ensure that *all* of ODESSA's elite members follow the leader.

Kip sees all this. He breaks away from the crowd that now disperses toward the main church entrance behind him. Kip moves forward, finding a place behind a pillar, trying to watch Rafe's departure with the Elect into the vestry. Doctor Damarung nearly knocks Kip over on his way out of the church. The good Doctor, now in high umbrage, does not notice the unfamiliar lab tech.

On the Abbey grounds at the exterior crypt doors

Marcy and Trevor look out onto the dark Abbey grounds; unknown country to Marcy and bad memories for Trevor. Marcy holds the end of a large chain attached to a harness on her wolfman. Trevor tries to remember Kip's coaching on how to hunch like an animal. He tries a hunch that looks more like a squat. Hunching is an acquired art.

They head out onto the grounds of the Abbey.

Within the vestry

The Elect remove their vestments under Orlok's paternal eye. Orlok gives not a hint that anyone should bat an eye at the presence of the Archduke Kopopkin. Most natural thing in the world that he should be here.

Karl enters. He sees Rafe removing the vestments of high office and looks, let's call it *puzzled,* for lack of a strong enough word. Orlok just nods to Karl, a nod both sharing amazement and counseling patience.

Once his inner circle has disrobed, Orlok speaks, "A most enjoyable ceremony. Both grand and elegant. Now, gentlemen, if you will await me in the chantry where Karl has prepared sherry and schnapps, I shall join you anon."

Karl struggles against his incomprehension, but surely Orlok knows best, "If you will follow me gentlemen."

They follow the bruised-faced Karl; Rafe last in line. Orlok interposes himself between the last departing brother and Rafe. Bruno and Gunter move close behind Rafe, just to make matters clear. Count Orlok says, "I'm afraid I have other plans for you, my dear Archduke."

Rafe had a feeling that he might miss the sherry and schnapps.

Within the Abbey church – crypt entrance

The Cohens enter the church from the interior crypt entrance, commando style. Eyes darting, guns ready, tactical hand signs mapping routes to cover. The IDF Commando would be proud. Ehud and Ezra take the lead, Hadassah and Papa close behind. They position themselves in places of concealment among the small arched chapels along the walls. They wait for the remaining celebrants to depart by the far church doors.

Within the dungeon

Chris heads for the stairs to make his journey down to the

cave entrance. A thought occurs to him. He pauses. He turns back to look at the cages and their helpless occupants. The hairy-folk, quiet and fearful, stare at him. He returns to the cages and opens them, coaxing out the reluctant hairy-folk.

Chris, "Come on. Come on. Follow me."

The hairy-folk step warily out. Chris stands at the stairs, ready to head down. "Come on. Let's escape. Come on."

They look at him for a moment, then rush the stairs.

Chris, "Good! Good!"

In a mass they turn at the stairwell and head up the stairs.

Chris, "Wait! No! This way!"

They run out of sight up the dungeon stairs. As Katrina would say: uh oh. Chris sees two hairy-monkey-boys trailing behind the rest, ready to head upstairs themselves. He grabs them, one in each arm. "You two come with me." Chris heads down the stairs to freedom with the hairy-kids.

Within the Abbey church – crypt entrance

The Cohen's remain in hiding as the last Nazi leaves the church. With the enemy now dispersed and unsuspecting, the Cohen's prepare to lay their mines. Then they watch, with what amazement can be imagined, as a horde of hairy-folk exit the crypt entrance and disperse everywhere.

Hadassah shakes her head in disapproval. Interpol agents should not bring spouses to work.

Within the hallway at the novice quarters

Orlok leads Rafe through the ill-lit corridor. Bruno and Gunter bring up the rear. They walk down the hall of the second floor. The floor without the gift shop. Rafe passes a cell barred by a stout plank augmenting its lock. The door rattles violently.

Count Orlok explains, "A special cell. Perhaps when we have completed your interrogation, I might introduce you to its occupant." Bruno and Gunter give the cell door a wide berth as they pass. Orlok arrives at a door to a different cell.

Bruno hurries to unlock it.

Count Orlok, "Your quarters. Excellency."

Rafe does not exactly show enthusiasm for going in.

Count Orlok, "I must now drink," he shudders, "schnapps … with the," this part comes hard, "rest … of the Elect." Strange times we live in. "After which I will repair to my study for a bit of cognac and muse on the evening's triumphs." Orlok luxuriates in the thought. "You will await me here, where tomorrow your interrogation shall begin in earnest."

Rafe, "I don't suppose you would be at home to considering how moved I was to be inducted into the Elect? Share a cognac together perhaps?"

Orlok frowns and points languidly to the cell, "Bruno." Bruno gives Rafe a hard shove into the cell.

Rafe, "Do I get to keep the robes? And shouldn't I have a medal, or a special hat or something?" Bruno locks him in.

Count Orlok, to Bruno, "Hold him fast until relieved." Orlok departs. We watch him proceed down the hall to the exit. And by "we" I mean you and I, dear reader, but also:

Kip, peering around the corner, watching Orlok exit with Gunter. Bruno stands his watch. Kip gathers his nerve, puts his hands into the pockets of his lab coat, and heads toward Bruno. Bruno sees him approaching, but Bruno does not deign to distinguish one lab tech from another.

Kip, "Hello Bruno. I'm here with the scopolamine."

Bruno does not understand.

Kip, "The truth serum. Count Orlok wants the prisoner softened up a little for the morning."

Bruno softens a bit.

Kip, "I'm Doctor Damarung."

Too far.

Kip, "Junior. Doctor Damarung Junior."

Well, Bruno guesses anyone could have a son. He opens the cell. Bruno follows Kip into the room. Rafe looks up at his visitors. Words cannot describe Rafe's expression, but let's

148

try these: mouth gapping, head slightly ajar, eyes straining as if he could somehow gain better focus that way. As if he lacks focus, when clarity of sight serves more as problem than solution.

Kip smiles. A friendly, warm smile to accompany, and perhaps soften—one might hope—the jarring incomprehension that his sudden appearance, in a lab coat, accompanied by Bruno, provokes. "Good evening, Mr. Archduke Riley. I'm here with your scopolamine."

This introduction does nothing to aid Rafe's struggle against insanity. Could Natasha have disguised herself as Kip? Nonsense, completely different shape. And why would she do such a thing? Could Kip have been disguising himself as Natasha all along? One could imagine Kip doing something like that. Just like him.

Kip, to Bruno, "Bruno, if you would roll up the prisoner's sleeve, please." Bruno bends over to do this as Rafe meekly offers his arm, eyes never leaving Kip. Probably Kip. Definitely not Natasha, so probably Kip. Or a cunning plan by Orlok. Perhaps a good shot of scopolamine will sort this all out.

Kip pantomimes bashing someone over the head. This makes about as much sense to Rafe as anything else does right now.

Kip, "Oh Bruno, I have a have a flower for you." A puzzled Bruno turns to face Kip. Rafe hits Bruno over the head. Bruno turns to face Rafe. Kip hits him the same. Bruno grows angry and turns to face Kip. Rafe lets go on Bruno's head with all the force his incipient insanity can muster. Bruno finally goes down.

Kip, "I've come to rescue you. Unless you've joined the Nazis, in which case I place you under arrest."

Rafe reaches out his hand, tentatively. He places it on Kip's chest. Rafe says, "Real."

Kip, "I know just how you feel, but we should probably talk on the run. Think you would fit into his outfit?"

Rafe decides fainting won't help and concentrates on present necessities, "I don't need a disguise, they all take me for an Archduke." They hear a noise in the hallway. "But who knows how long that will hold up."

They exit to the hallway, Kip still a lab tech, Rafe still a Duke. They take off down the hall. Passing close to the barred cell they hear a rumble from within and jump back.

Rafe, "Let's get anywhere but here."

They leave the second floor of the novices' quarters by a door. The rattling of the cell door dies down and all returns to quiet. Then one of the escaped dungeon creatures walks down the hall. A hairy-wolf-man, meek and shuffling, passes by the barred cell. Noises again emerge from behind the barred cell door. The hairy-wolf-man looks at the door. He hears a loud *squawk* from the cell and jumps back. The hairy-wolf-man sniffs the air. He starts to shake. His body contorts. His limbs grow. He transforms before our eyes into a proper werewolf, fangs and all.

Bruno staggers out of the cell where once he kept Rafe, holding his sore head. The werewolf looks at him with vicious eyes. The werewolf attacks him.

Poor Bruno.

On the Abbey grounds

Rafe and Kip speed-walk the Abbey grounds, trying to stay in the dark, which they do, and to keep cool heads, which proves harder.

Rafe, "What are you doing here?"

Kip, "Rescuing you."

Rafe, "I mean what brought you here?"

Kip, "The same thing that brought you here."

Rafe, "Okay. What am I doing here?"

Kip, "Searching for Formula XOX." They hug the outer church wall to stay out of the light.

Rafe, "Formula what?"

Kip, "XOX."

Rafe, "I never heard of such a thing."

Kip will work the problem, "Did you come looking for Nazis?"

Rafe, "No. I found Nazis; I did not look for them. No one could have been as surprised as I to find Nazis."

Kip, "Were you looking for Marcy?"

Rafe grows irritated, "No, that was all a mistake! Marcy isn't here. She has nothing to do with this." They hear brown-shirt men singing a drinking song. They freeze. Rafe grabs Kip and steers him into the cloister.

The cloister

Marcy and Trevor walk the covered square of the cloister grounds, dimly lit by the small and occasional lights from the overhanging cover of the walkway. They walk slowly so as not to call attention to themselves. Why a woman walking her werewolf in an abbey cloister high in the Andes would be better concealed by slow rather than rapid ambulation they have not theorized on, but as they lack any obvious place to go, slow seems right anyway.

Trevor, "We need to do something to accelerate our search as I am not at all confident that your Israeli Commandos mean to delay their immolation of the Abbey."

Marcy, "We could split up."

Trevor, "You, a woman alone in a monastery, and I, an escaped werewolf? That sounds a right invitation to a blow on the head."

Marcy makes a quick survey of the terrain. She sees two men walking the cloister opposite them. One seems faintly reminiscent of Rafe, but of course *he* could not be here. "The darkness plays tricks on the eyes." She glances across the courtyard again, but the men have moved past her now.

The cloister – still

Rafe and Kip walk the cloister trying to look casual.

Kip, "The formula can no longer be written down. It's a

distilled virus. In its natural form the virus causes weakness and passivity. Distilled it must make people catatonic!"

Rafe, "And they have it here? In the Abbey?"

Kip, "I'm sure of it. I'm mostly sure of it. That Bruno fellow recognized the name of Doctor Damarung, so he at least must be here."

Rafe stops in his tracks, "Doctor Damarung! He must be stopped at the coast! It all makes sense now!"

Kip can hardly wait to hear.

Rafe, "No. No it doesn't. It still makes no sense at all." They walk again.

Kip, "I'm telling you we need to find the formula!"

Rafe, "*Can* you find it?"

Kip, "I can find the lab. Follow me."

They exit the cloister.

The cloister – yet still

Marcy walks the cloister next to Trevor.

Marcy, "We need a better plan."

Trevor, "We need better means to carry out a plan. We are possessed of pluck and gumption, while we greatly need speed and stealth."

From above a ninja-quality drop takes out Trevor. Knocks him cold; right out. Natasha rears a fist back to take out her second opponent, who raises an arm to block her. They both freeze.

Really freeze. Dead stop.

Natasha, "Marcy?"

Marcy blinks, "Natasha?"

Natasha looks at the form at her feet, "I have saved you from a beast."

Marcy, "Trevor!" Marcy takes a knee to pick up the fallen Trevor.

Natasha, "Trevor?" Natasha bends down to lend aid.

Trevor comes around. He shakes his head. He looks at Marcy, "Mother?"

Natasha inspects poor Trevor, "Trevor. Fear not, we will find a cure!"

Marcy, "It's just makeup. He wears it to blend in."

Natasha considers the logic of this, "A profound error or a brilliant mis-direction."

They hoist Trevor to his feet. He stands unsteadily between them. He comes round a bit. He says, "I really do think I might just sit this one out." He notices who holds him. "Natasha! Thank god."

Natasha, "I am here to help you Trevor."

Trevor, "We seek Kip, lost on the grounds, and the Formula XOX, and now the vile blaggard who keeps dropping on me from above and knocking me senseless."

Marcy looks awkwardly at her feet.

Natasha, "I will avenge you. What is Formula XOX?"

Marcy, "Don't get him started on that."

Trevor, "Aren't you here for the secret formula?"

Natasha, "I search for Rafe."

Marcy, "Rafe?"

Trevor, "Rafe?"

They hear someone approaching on the cloister path.

Natasha, "We will search for our missing puppies. You two search the cable car to the east. I will cover the south and west of the Abbey. We will meet at the library on the northeast, where I do not think these here will look for us. Can you do this?"

They nod.

Natasha, "Take this." She hands Marcy the gun recently removed from a guard.

Marcy, "Don't you need a weapon?"

Natasha, "I am my weapon. We go."

They go.

Outside the Abbey laboratory

Rafe and Kip stand at the door to the lab. Kip keeps his eyes up scanning the heavens above.

Rafe, "What are you doing?"

Kip, "The sky falls around here."

Rafe glances up. The sky appears as stable as always. The heavenly spheres turn slowly, making the music only philosophers can hear. Or perhaps the world turns as the cross remains steady. In either case, nothing falls. Rafe considers the door of the lab before them. A question of protocol arises.

Rafe, "Do we knock?"

Kip jumps back.

Within the Abbey laboratory

Kip and Rafe walk through the sea of tinted bottles and obsolescent electronics. They slowly make their way to the back of the lab.

Kip whispers, "Have we found a lab or an antique shop?"

Rafe whispers, "How do we find an XOX? Will it be marked on a bottle? Do we do a taste test?"

Kip considers, "It would look or smell Germanic maybe."

Rafe turns to him, "How does that narrow anything down?"

Kip, "I don't know. It's not a normal secret formula. It can no longer be written down. Maybe is smells like something."

They reach the rear of the lab. They see a single stunted man in an antique lab coat weeping at a table, his back to them. His shoulders shake as tears roll down his cheeks.

Kip makes a bold guess, "Doctor Damarung?"

The man turns. He looks just as Kip had always pictured the mad scientist. Add his picture to the encyclopedia under that heading. Damarung replies, "Yes?"

Rafe, to Kip, "After all this, I expected something more—I don't know—terrifying."

Kip, to Damarung, "Doctor Damarung *Senior*?"

A puzzled look from the good doctor; irritation from Rafe.

Damarung shows a bit of recognition through his bitter tears and well gnashed teeth. Squinting through his glasses, he addresses Rafe, "Archduke Kopopkin?"

Rafe sighs heavily. How does he always manage to get stuck with the first thought that crosses his mind? Rafe says, "Yes. I am the Archduke."

Damarung's hopes grow, "You belong to the Elect now."

Rafe, "Yes. I do. I have my badge here somewhere." Rafe searches his person.

Damarung stands and quickly approaches Rafe. He takes hold of Rafe's lapels, "Seize the moment! Depose Orlok! Bring our work to fruition!"

Rafe pulls Damarung's hands off his coat. Herr Doctor calms slightly. Rafe says, "Interesting notion. I can see the need for a coup. Past time really. ODESSA seems out of date to say the least."

Kip, "And evil."

Rafe shoots Kip his *let me do this* look. "Not that you don't mean well. Just maybe need a top to bottom rethink. Reassess first principles."

Doctor Damarung nods excitedly, "Exactly! We have lost our way!" Damarung's voice trembles with the terrible truth of this.

Rafe, "Right. Very much to tell the truth. Still, even now, you can get in touch with your essential humanity."

Doctor Damarung, "We can do better than humanity!"

Rafe, "Yes. Well that might be more a source of the problem than a solution."

Rafe searches for a properly inspiring message, and happens upon something he read in an in-flight magazine once, "Transform your world by transforming yourself."

Damarung listens with great care, "But what of the traitor Orlok?"

Rafe pulls from the same source of inspiration, "An enemy is just a friend you haven't met yet."

Kip tries his hand, "A friend is another self."

Rafe, "Kip, if you don't mind." But then he thinks, "No, actually that's a good one." To Damarung, "A friend is another self of yours."

Damarung turns away, deep in thought, "Yes. I begin to see."

Kip attempts to get things back on track, "You might make a start by handing us Formula XOX."

Rafe nods. Good start that.

Damarung begins a mad laugh. "Hahahahahaha!!!" The man does a great mad laugh. "You wouldn't long have hands if I did. Hahahahaha!!!"

Rafe and Kip try to chuckle along with this. Rafe, "Ha, ha. Very funny. No hands." Rafe makes the cuckoo bird sign to Kip.

Doctor Damarung, "But with Orlok in command how can we do this? And what shall we use as a suitable vessel?"

Rafe doesn't follow, "Orlok?"

Doctor Damarung, "Orlok?"

Rafe, "Orlok isn't suitable for command. We can take charge, you and I, and retire Orlok to turning pages in the Holy of Holies."

Kip loses the train of things here.

Rafe, "Then you hand—give—give us the formula and—"

The light has gone off for Damarung, it glows a thousand watts strong, "Yes! Yes! You have solved the riddle!"

Rafe looks pleased. He solved the riddle without even knowing it existed. That shows skill. Natasha will be very impressed when she hears.

Doctor Damarung, "For years I have been injecting him with revitalizing fluid. The effect of transformation upon him would be incalculable." Words could hardly describe the evil glee with which Doctor Damarung completes this thought, "He would be a most suitable vessel."

Rafe sees he has made a convert, "Oh, the best vessel. Clearly."

Doctor Damarung, "And by using Orlok we then would—how does the old saying go? Kill two Jews with one stone."

Rafe, disturbed, "That's not how the saying goes."

Kip, "No."

Doctor Damarung moves with purpose to the table. He opens a drawer and pulls out a large key which he puts into his pocket, and a large gun which he points at Rafe and Kip. Doctor Damarung does not intend to trust fine words anymore. He announces, "Orlok will soon return to his study to take his leisure and drink his cognac. I shall retrieve the formula, as you call it. You will go now to the Abbey library and detain Orlok. I will meet you there." Damarung looks well past reasoning with now. He grabs two shackles with long chains from the table and throws them at the feet of Kip and Rafe. "Take these! We will need to restrain Orlok during the moment of the Great Awakening!"

Rafe and Kip look at Damarung's gun, then down at the chains.

Outside the Abbey laboratory

Rafe and Kip leave the lab, chains in hand, not exactly flushed with victory, but who can tell in the dark? Someone watches them from the corner of the building as they depart.

Rafe, "That went well. I think."

Kip, "He promised us Formula XOX."

Rafe, "Did that happen?"

They move on towards the library at the opposite end of the Abbey. Ehud watches them go. He straps a stack of dynamite onto the building. Doctor Damarung leaves the lab. He heads toward the novice's quarters holding a gun and a key. Ezra watches him go.

Ehud and Ezra plant bombs on the lab.

Outside the cable car facility

Marcy gropes her way in the dark. Moonlight might brighten a country meadow, but it offers sparse help blocked by the Abbey's massive stonework. So she gropes as she goes. Then she touches something. "There you are. I can't see a thing. I think I need to break our no flashlight rule."

She turns on her flashlight, illuminating a hairy-man-dog. She jumps back. "Oh my god!" She jumps into another hairy figure and jumps back again. Her light reveals Trevor.

Marcy, "Trevor!"

Trevor, "I must say, we would be better served with less exclamation."

Marcy, "I saw a hairy man on the loose!"

Trevor, "I've seen them too. They roam the grounds, out and about on their own. Someone must have freed them from their cages."

Marcy, "What idiot would do that?"

They press on.

Within the Abbey church

Rafe and Kip press tight against a column listening to sounds further in the church. Rafe peers around the column. He sees a large, bearded man in a kippah and a young woman armed with two semi-automatic pistols. They secure dynamite to the walls.

Kip, whispering, "What do you see?"

Rafe rubs his eyes and looks again.

Kip, whispering louder, "Well?"

Rafe, "A rabbi planting bombs."

The idea scores high on poetic justice but low on *meets expectations*. Kip, "Let's *not* cut through the church."

Rafe nods.

Outside the laboratory

Ehud and Ezra stand exposed in a yellow over-head light while adjusting radio detonators. Dieter and Johan walk near and see them. Two young men in khaki wearing kippahs at the lab. Dieter feels like the Nazi gods have provided a night's vacation entertainment. He shouts with sadistic glee. "Juden!"

Ehud and Ezra turn and level their submachine guns at them.

Panic. Dieter, "Armed Juden!"

The two Nazis flee. Ehud and Ezra watch the Nazis flee. They do not follow. The Jewish Guerrilla Assault Force stays mission focused. Ehud speaks briefly into his two-way radio. They resume planting bombs.

Outside the Abbey charter house

Rafe and Kip press against the rounded wall of the charter house. Rafe peers over one of the building's ornamental mini-buttresses to find the source of a noise. Rafe looks and sees: a proper werewolf, snout still covered in Bruno's blood.

Kip, whispers, "What do you see?"

Rafe drops down. He stares off into the night stars, "I must be asleep. On scopolamine. Something." Rafe knocks his forehead against the stone and looks round the buttress again. He drops back to the wall. "Nope. Still there."

Kip, "What? What do you see?"

Admitting insanity comes hard. Finding no other word, Rafe shrugs, "A werewolf."

Kip jumps up and past their cover, "That's Trevor!"

Even in the context of following the orders of a mad scientist, while sneaking about on a Nazi monastery, about to be blown up by a rabbi, having just seen a werewolf, this takes Rafe by surprise. Kip runs toward the werewolf. Rafe remains surprised.

Kip, "Trevor you old dog!" Kip offers his hand to the blood-soaked werewolf as to an old friend well met. Werewolves do not have old friends so naturally (if that is the right word for it) the werewolf attacks. It leaps at Kip with a snarl. Kip notices that this is a very non-Trevor like behavior. Kip back peddles, shocked.

A werewolf attack—as opposed to, say, a werewolf handshake—makes sense, so Rafe can handle this. Rafe rushes the beast and beats it back with the shackles provided earlier by Doctor Damarung. He tosses a chain to Kip who lays into the werewolf. The beast scuttles and howls, perfectly normal behavior in a werewolf. It lashes out in retreat. Both men chain-whip the beast until at last they can break free of the fight.

Rafe, "Run!"

Kip does not need to be told twice to flee an attacking werewolf. They run.

Within the Abbey novice quarters

Doctor Damarung approaches the barred cell. He carries shackle and chain over his shoulders. He removes the wooden bar that blocks the large oak door. The Beast in the Cell grows excited, judging from its sounds. Shuffling and scratching, with the odd *squawk* thrown in.

Doctor Damarung, "Patience my pretty. Patience. Father has come for you."

More scratching and soft *kwit-kwit-kwit* sound behind the door.

Doctor Damarung unlocks the door, "Patience my pretty." Damarung enters the cell.

Within the Abbey charter house

Behold again the inner sanctum, the Holy of Holies, with its Nazi decor of swastika flags, Hitler busts, Fuhrer art, wreath-gripping German eagles, shirtless male Olympians in mid man-pose. Illuminated at its alter rests the vat containing Hitler's brain. The Fuhrer's portrait now hangs above it, his name and title embossed in bronze on the bottom of the vat.

And standing at the entrance, Papa Cohen and Hadassah, incongruous amongst the Nazi regalia. They approach the Fuhrer vat, with expressions well past curious but held short of aghast by a good helping of *no way*.

Hadassah slowly draws her .45. She levels it at the vat and its brain within the glass. The muzzle of Hadassah's gun presses against the vat, level with the eyes. The eyes don't open wide, since they have no lids, but let's just say: they notice. If ever the brain swelled with excitement, this would be the time.

Papa Cohen puts his hand on Hadassah's gun. He lowers it. Hadassah looks at Papa Cohen. He shakes his head to her: No.

Within the Abbey library

The Master's study, his collection of books and fine furnishings. Rather more Nazified than he prefers, but still his private inner sanctum. Alone here, Rafe and Kip, disheveled but unharmed, stand at a desk. Two shackles drape a chair next to them.

Rafe, "What I cannot fathom, which is to say, the first among the many things I cannot fathom, is how you mistook that," he collects himself, "werewolf, for Trevor."

Kip, "It looked just like him. In the dark."

Rafe, "It looked like a werewolf!"

Kip, "That's what I'm saying."

Rafe, "To start with, I don't think you're shocked enough that we just encountered a werewolf."

Kip, "Old hat for me." Kip thinks a moment, "They're usually pretty shy though. Tame would be putting it mildly."

Rafe stares incredulously, but this does not seem to shake Kip's confidence.

Kip, "And frankly I think Trevor looks more convincing. Not to toot my own horn."

Rafe, "Of course not."

Kip, "I mean I've seen a few by now."

Rafe, "Werewolves."

Kip, "And Trevor is one of the best. Not to toot my own horn."

Rafe rubs his temples. Somewhere, somehow, the briefing system broke down. His own detection ability failed him. He followed a red herring, over a cliff, into a paradox, buried in a labyrinth. The world—his niche of it anyway— stopped making sense. Somewhere in all this, a message lies; probably encrypted, and best ignored. Rafe has the distinct feeling that the foundational cause of all of his perplexity lies precisely in his effort the make the blizzard of confusion that constitutes reality into some ordered sense. Where did Orlok keep the cognac?

The library door creaks closed, pushed by a draft; a disturbing sound to Kip and Rafe since they closed it when they entered. Firmly closed doors, even at a werewolf abbey, don't re-close on their own. The two men look to the door. It's entrance lies shaded by the stone arch of the room. From the shadows of the library entryway, Count Orlok emerges, holding a luger on the two adventurers.

Count Orlok, "Gentlemen. I have you now." Orlok walks toward them. "You shall not escape me this time. Though I do acknowledge that you possess an impressive talent for evasion. You are a more worthy advisory than I had anticipated. Every word a chess move. I will not again underestimate you my dear Archduke."

Rafe, annoyed, "I abdicate as Archduke. The aristocracy has been nothing but a pain in my ass since I joined. You may have it all to yourself Count."

Orlok looks at Kip. Doctor Damarung might have grown too excited to track lab staffing anomalies, but Count Orlok keeps up to date on anything presenting as an item on his budget. He has not budgeted for this stranger. Orlok gives Kip a look inviting explanation.

Kip, "Oh. Sorry. Kip Carson, conceptual artist."

On the list of items that Field Marshal Count Frederick Adolphus von Orlok, Superior of the Abbey of the Eagles and Commander of the Organization of Former SS Officers (Descendent) has neither previously encountered, nor ever thought to encounter, a conceptual artist portraying a laboratory technician, conspiring with a member of the Russian aristocracy—newly abdicated—in Orlok's own study, must rank high. And to encounter a conceptual artist thus occupied, and in such circumstances, might derail any ordinary third generation Andean Mountain secret society evil cult leader. But to his credit, Orlok maintains the poise and self-possession that marks him out as belonging to the first rank of super-villainy. Though he does note to himself how many novel occurrences this quinquennial meeting of ODESSA has brought. An event surely to take a prominent place in his memoirs.

Orlok motions Rafe and Kip away from the desk as he comes to stand behind it. "In any event, I now have you both. And in the fullness of time, I shall have the woman as well."

Kip, "Woman?"

Finally Rafe knows something that someone else doesn't. Rafe says to Kip, "I have my secrets too."

Count Orlok, "Soon you will have no secrets from me."

The library door creaks. All the men look to the arch-darkened library entrance. Marcy speaks from the shadows, "Drop the gun mister! I have you now." Marcy emerges from the dark of the library entry holding the gun Natasha provided. Orlok drops his gun on the desk.

Count Orlok, "I prefer *Count*."

Rafe looks stunned—even more so than has been usual of late, "Marcy?"

Kip gets it now, "Oh, *that* woman. You found Marcy."

Rafe, "I did? I mean, apparently, I have." Amazed and proud all at once, "I rescued Marcy!" Natasha will be so impressed when she hears.

While Rafe looks pleased with himself, Orlok looks puzzled. How badly did he miscount visitors on the Abbey tour? Trevor enters from the shadows behind Marcy carrying his chain.

Rafe, "Marcy look out! Behind you! A werewolf!"

Kip puts a calming arm on Rafe's shoulder, "That's Trevor."

Rafe cannot understand Kip's werewolf/Trevor delusion. Rafe, to Kip, "Have you gone mad?"

Trevor, "I say, it is a bloody irritation having to explain myself so often. Not to mention the interminable itching."

Okay, that must be Trevor. Rafe says, "My god. Trevor's been turned into a werewolf!" No one really feels up to briefing Rafe on this right now. Marcy and Trevor come near.

Marcy, "All right Count," wondering a moment, "whoever you are. I place you under arrest for..." Marcy now encounters some of the subtle difficulties arising from the need to draw up a charge list for all this. "For werewolf kidnapping and ... alpaca murder and ... failure to properly register an abbey." That should just about cover. For now. Rafe scratches his head, and even Orlok looks a bit perplexed.

Rafe suggests an addition, sure to figure prominently at trial, "And they saved Hitler's brain."

Incredulous looks all around. Except for Orlok, who nevertheless strikes an expression meant to encourage skepticism on this point.

Rafe, "No, really, I saw it."

Orlok takes the high road, "Frankly, all this has the appearance of the impromptu. I suggest we all sit. I will serve a round of port, and we can come to terms, like gentlemen." He notices an immediate problem with the suggestion. He nods to Marcy, "My lady."

A round on the house sounds fine to Rafe, but that opportunity passes.

The library door creaks again. A new figure emerges from the shadows.

Karl von Hapen shouts, "No one move! I have you now!" Karl enters from the darkness of the library doorway. Dressed in his Gestapo black and armed with the standard issue Abbey luger. (You can buy these in the gift shop by the way.) Karl says to Marcy, "Put down that gun." She drops her gun.

Count Orlok, "Excellent. Karl." Orlok reaches for his pistol.

Karl, "Do not move Herr Count! Not until I find out *exactly* what goes on here."

The Count stops, but nothing stops Rafe, "It's simple Karl. My colleagues and I," He indicates Kip, Marcy, and, well, the werewolf next to her. Trevor nods to Karl. "Have just uncovered a plot against the Fuhrer's ... brain. I had just put Count Orlok under arrest when you came in."

Orlok comes close to losing his imperturbable detachment, "This is preposterous!" Now for all his faults, Orlok has a very good point here.

Karl, "Silence!" To Rafe, "What plot?"

Rafe shines in moments like these, "Count Orlok here has a secret formula," Rafe glances at Kip. Thanks for this one buddy, "Formula X." A promising start. But where now? Rafe struggles on, "And, uh, he uses this to create weak werewolves," a nod to Trevor. "And he uses these weak werewolves to make stronger werewolves. And when he has one strong enough—a suitable vessel you might say," the key here, Rafe knows: work in everything you've heard, "then, with these, he will, um, he will," inspiration strikes, "he will transplant Hitler's brain into it! And Hitler will have a body. Of a werewolf. And thus, Orlok will finally resolve the brain thing. And then," endings are so hard, "ODESSA will go on to rule the world!"

Silence. Dead, absolute, silence.

Karl breaks the quiet of the room, "Ja, everyone knows this."

Well, not quite everyone. Rafe says, "That's real? All real?"

Orlok smiles. He has always appreciated the advantage of advancing a sinister plot no sane person could credit. He feels again in command of the room. Until...

The library door creaks.

Natasha emerges, "Drop your weapon Nazi thug, I have you now."

Karl, "Agent Raskalitkanof? But you are one of us. A loyal servant of ODESSA. Under the direction of Herr Fuchs, no?"

Marcy cocks her head in confusion. It occurs to her that she has missed more briefings on this mission than a good supervisor should. Rafe notices her confusion and just shrugs at her. Of course this mission doesn't make sense to anyone. How much sympathy can he have for her though? After all, she entered the room leading a werewolf.

Natasha addresses Karl's concern, "I will arrest Herr Fuchs in good time. Drop your weapon."

Karl knows a thing or two about deadly eyes, and this woman clearly has them. Karl drops his weapon as Natasha emerges from the darkened entryway.

Kip grows very excited at this turn of events, "It's Natasha! Rafe, look! Natasha! Do you see this? Who would have expected her?"

Count Orlok's day has flipped on him again, "Unbelievable!"

Natasha moves into the room, backing Karl away from his pistol.

Natasha, "I am officially arresting those I am not rescuing."

Marcy does a head count and a quick calculation, "Well, I think this is everybody."

Not quite. The library door creaks. From the shadow of the entry emerges the menacing figure of Doctor Damarung, cast in lunacy by the lights, holding a gun in one hand and a chain in the other.

Doctor Damarung, "We have you now."

Natasha drops a nightstick, her only weapon. All watch as Doctor Damarung enters into the light. From the shadows behind him, at the end of the chain, a beast. Part man; part eagle. A man's face with a bird's beak. Legs with claws for feet. Human hands at the bend of its wings. It stands five feet tall. A thing from a damned world.

It squawks. A terrifying sound.

Out on the Abbey grounds

Submachine-gun bursts flash in the night. Bullets ricochet off stone walls. The sound of gunfire echoes in the high mountains. The acoustics of stone being what they are, and the windows of the Abbey being rather narrow as a rule, one could only guess what those inside a building hear, but the mountains echo the drama.

Ehud and Ezra take turns letting off controlled bursts at frightened Nazis. The Argentine Zionist Commando comes alive with action. They make their way back to the outer crypt entrance; satchels empty of explosives. They take turns firing at the Nazis as they make their way.

Nazis flee.

Within the upper cable car room

A brown-shirt worker sits reading the latest issue of *Uniforms and Insignia Monthly*. (Great cover story on placement of specialty badges for noncommissioned officers of the Wehrmacht circa 1940.) He hears a popping sound off in the distance. He reluctantly lowers the magazine.

Into the room bursts one of the ODESSA Elect, "Israeli Paratroopers attack the Abbey! Hundreds of them!" The worker jumps up to attention.

The ODESSA Elect-man barks orders, "Hand out lugers! Bring up the cable cars! ODESSA Elect members escape first!"

The worker works the cable car levers. The engine hums loudly. Giant wheels pull threaded steel ropes to the sound of antiquated machinery. It promises to be, at best, a slow and noisy escape.

On the grounds at the exterior crypt doors

Ehud and Ezra fire bursts into the night. They reload ammo clips and fire again. They make deliberate progress toward the doors to the crypt stairs.

A final burst from Ezra, he passes through the doors to exit into the crypt entrance and down the stairs.

A final burst from Ehud. He follows.

No Nazi pursues.

Within the Abbey library

Doctor Damarung, armed with gun and were-eagle, steps

toward the throng before him. They part, revealing a slightly nervous Count Orlok. The were-eagle shrieks like a harpy from the netherworld. It squawks like a damned thing from the lower hell. Its foul odor disperses throughout the room.

Count Orlok again tries to reassert control of the evening, "Very good Doctor Damarung. And you have brought our friend. Very good." Orlok's tone suggests a more ambivalent attitude towards the presence of their "friend."

Doctor Damarung and his were-eagle pass Natasha and Karl. Natasha eyes the gun on the ground, everyone else just moves out of the way of the mad doctor and the foul, screeching beast. Karl, more knowing of the creature's nature than the others, has taken the only action appropriate and peed his SS pants.

Count Orlok, "Perhaps. Perhaps one of our new guests will prove the suitable vessel we have so long sought. That would be grand, to have a suitable vessel at last."

Marcy and Trevor move aside as the two pass them. Marcy, not yet truly adjusted to were-*wolves*, recalibrates her bestiary to include ones with beaks and feathers. Trevor wonders if were-beasts feel solidarity with one another. He hunches down a bit just in case.

Count Orlok, "And, of course, a special reward for you, so timely in your arrival. A promotion of course. General Doctor Damarung, High Priest of the Sacred Alter, perhaps? A vacation? New containers for your laboratory?"

Rafe and Kip distance themselves from the mad doctor and the screeching beast as they pass. Rafe eyes the gun on the desk that Damarung now stands before, which Orlok stands behind.

Count Orlok, "And, naturally, treats for your pet." One shudders to think what counts as a treat for a were-eagle.

No one speaks. An eerie silence prevails, disturbed only by the high-pitched squeaking noise of the were-eagle.

Damarung cracks the silence, "No, Herr Count. I shall not be delayed. Tonight, you fulfill your promise. And our destiny." Damarung looks at the were-eagle. It looks back at him, almost touchingly, like a child to its father. Doctor Damarung addresses the beast, "My pretty. My pretty!"

The beast grows excited.

Doctor Damarung, "My pretty!!!"

The best squawks furiously. It flaps its wings and claws at the floor.

Count Orlok, "Herr Doctor! Control the creature!"

Damarung turns and points to Orlok, "There he stands! There! There!"

Damarung drops the chain. The were-eagle leaps the table in a flapping of its wings, screeching a harpy's war cry. Claws out, it descends on the helpless Count Orlok. It lets out a terrible piercing sound as it lands on the defenseless Count. It tears and rends his flesh. It bites him savagely.

Orlok screams, "No! Noooooooo!!!"

Natasha knocks Karl out of the way and grabs his gun from the floor. She runs to the desk behind which the were-eagle attacks Orlok, before which Damarung watches with mad glee.

Rafe snatches Orlok's luger off the desk. Both Rafe and Natasha lean over the desk, each on either side of Damarung. They fire their guns at the were-eagle.

It squawks, hisses and writhes with the impact of the bullets. Natasha and Rafe slow their rate of fire, taking careful aim now. The were-eagle twists in agony and falls on the body of Orlok. It ceases to move.

Their guns empty, Rafe and Natasha lower their weapons. Damarung has dropped to the floor, kneeling, as if in prayer.

Trevor, Kip, and Marcy appear beside Rafe and Natasha.

Rafe, "I guess he didn't see that coming."

They look at the scene where a moment ago the were-eagle attacked Orlok. They see Orlok, dead eyes looking to the ceiling of his beloved library. A small, naked, dead man lies on top of him. Feathers drift in the draft all around.

Faintly, beyond the walls, the sound of guns firing.

Within the Abbey church at the crypt entrance

Brown-shirt Nazis make their way through the church, led by Dieter, luger in hand. They are mad for a fight. They mean to go all out in defense of their Abbey. Dieter sees Papa Cohen, he yells, "Juden!" Dieter sees Hadassah, his face forms a sadistic leer, "Junge judische Frau." Hadassah turns on them.

The eyes of Hadassah: she sees the advancing Nazis. Her eyes say: You do not want to mess with me.

Dieter smiles, "Get her!"

Some people just aren't paying attention.

Hadassah raises her two enormous pistols. She levels them at the Nazis. The muzzles flash. The guns of Hadassah speak Hebrew. They say: BANG. They say it over and over again. Shell casings and Nazis hit the ground. Then she stops. Hadassah holsters her guns. She turns, guns on hips, backpack full. She walks—she does not run—she walks, to the crypt stairs.

Dieter shouts, "She flees!"

Some people just aren't paying attention.

The Nazis rise from the floor. They look toward the crypt entrance. Papa Cohen comes into view.

Dieter, "Alter Jude!"

Papa Cohen raises his machine gun.

It goes: RAT-A-TAT-TAT. The muzzle flashes illuminate the face of Papa Cohen. Ferocious in the bursts of light. And to what effect? Let's just say it's a bad night to be a Nazi. Papa Cohen lowers his gun. He walks—he does not run—to the crypt stairs.

Within the Abbey library

The team, the Silencers, united at last. Hugs and pats on the back all around. Damarung weeps before the bodies of the once were-eagle and Orlok. Karl stands with the Silencers and looks on, confused but smiling; happy to be a part of the group in spite of his SS gear.

Kip, to Trevor, "You're alive! You're in one piece."

Trevor, to Kip, "I'm splendid! I've only been knocked unconscious thrice since I last saw you. Nothing to it anymore."

Natasha, to Rafe, "I have rescued you again."

Rafe, to her, "Took your sweet time about it."

Natasha, "It would have been easier if you had stayed in your cell."

Rafe, "I knew you Russians like a challenge." Rafe nods at Trevor, "Do we have a cure for that?"

Natasha, "I have not been entirely briefed."

Rafe, "Did you see that I found Marcy?"

Natasha, "I sent her to you."

Karl watches, enjoying the fellowship and good cheer. So wonderful to be one among others.

Kip, to Marcy, "How did you get here?"

Marcy, "Underground. You?"

Kip, "Flew like an eagle. A metaphorical one."

Marcy, to Rafe, "And you?"

Rafe, "Tourist."

Marcy points to Damarung, still on his knees and weeping, she asks Trevor, "So that's Damarung?"

Trevor, "Haven't yet had the pleasure. Too busy pulling myself up off the ground."

Kip, "That's him. We spoke. Not such a bad guy. Misguided, obviously."

Marcy, "And the silver haired fellow? Who was he?"

Rafe fields this one, "Count Orlok. Head Nazi."

Marcy, "I see." She points to Karl, "Then who is *he*?"

Everyone goes silent and looks at Karl.

He smiles at them for a moment, and then realizes it's his turn. He straightens to attention. "Karl von Hapen, your prisoner." He clicks his heels.

Marcy remembers something, "We need to make for the exit. I'll call this in and lead us out." Talk picks up again as Marcy works the walkie-talkie, "We are all clear. Five friendlies and one prisoner coming out now."

Rafe, to Natasha, "So I suppose you've been dropping Nazis all over the place."

Natasha, "Yes. Mostly Nazis."

Rafe, "I fought off a werewolf."

Natasha, "I as well, sort of."

As they speak grouped before the desk, behind them, where they do not look, a pair of wings appears. Yes, wings. Large ones. The wings grow larger still. They stretch and expand. They shake and rattle. The wings, with feathers like razors and human hands at their joints, expand silently behind the desk and before the weeping Doctor Damarung. They become enormous. The wings reach to the ceiling. The hands at the bend of the wings grow claws from fingers. A head appears. The head and beak of an eagle, the face of Orlok.

Doctor Damarung weeps not tears of grief, but tears of joy. A suitable vessel at last. The great were-eagle continues to grow.

Marcy lowers the walkie-talkie and turns to the group, "Switch thrown. Fifteen minutes to doomsday. We should—" She stops abruptly, seeing the horror behind them. A great screech erupts from the Orlok were-eagle.

Doctor Damarung exults, "Behold the Blood of the Beast!"

And behold they do. Holy crap. The were-eagle rises. Six feet. Seven feet. The Silencers look on, dumbfounded. Karl too, for that matter. Marcy looks around the floor for the gun she dropped. The were-eagle grows. Nine feet. And none too happy. Orlok-the-were-eagle wears a face of panic. The unflappable Count now counts as thoroughly flapped. And indeed its wings do so. Beaks can't smile or frown, but the rest of Orlok's face suggests that he did not plan to spend his evening this way.

Marcy sees the gun she dropped on the floor and goes for it.

Doctor Damarung shouts to Rafe and Kip, "The chains! We must bind the beast and make ready the Great Transformation! Grab the chains!"

In an instant Rafe and Kip lunge for the chains. Marcy picks up the luger. Natasha snatches up a candelabra, the only non-Nazi blunt object in view—Orlok must have loved this item.

Orlok-the-were-eagle lets loose a hellish noise. It flexes its new avian muscles. It overturns the desk. It bounds toward the great fireplace. Its joint-of-the-wings hands grasp at the fireplace mantle. Its wings flap the air straining to fly.

Rafe and Kip dare the threat of the giant claws on its feet to attach leg-irons. Were-eagle-Orlok, still in the emotional adjustment period of were-beast conversion, offers only token resistance to Rafe and Kip. They snap the manacles closed. They have chained the were-eagle—to nothing. What now?

Doctor Damarung, "We must drag it to the lab!"

Not that. Doctor Damarung must have a radically defective sense of current events if he thinks anyone will drag a nine-foot crazed were-Orlok anyplace.

Marcy takes a shot with the pistol. She misses as the round dings off the wall next to the were-eagle. Panicked before, this sends it over the edge. It shakes loose Rafe and Kip with a powerful thrust of its legs and half climbs, half flies, up the mantle. It crests the mantle and comes face to face with the image above it. It takes one look at the picture of Adolph Hitler and, out of panic or anger who can tell, begins to rip it to shreds with its claws.

Rafe and Kip grab the chains. Trevor joins on Kip's chain. They yank the were-eagle hard from the mantle as Marcy's second shot misses. The were-eagle lands just before Doctor Damarung.

Doctor Damarung, "My pretty!"

Wrong were-eagle. The were-Orlok bites Damarung's head, covering the head entirely with its beak. It picks

Damarung up, shakes him about and spits him out. body first, then the head. No more Doctor Damarung.

Natasha strikes the were-eagle hard in the head with the candelabra. It looks at her weapon. Is that longing in its eyes? A shot rings out and grazes the were-eagle's head. It turns and charges at Marcy. Natasha joins on the chain with Rafe to slow it down.

Karl grabs the gun from Marcy, pushing her down. He cries at the were-Orlok: "I live to serve you, Master!"

The were-eagle makes it to Karl, dragging people from its chains. It clutches Karl's throat with its wing-hands and lifts him up. Karl chokes and so can no longer profess, or amend, his loyalties. The beast snaps Karl's neck. No more Karl.

The were-eagle leaps, shaking off its handlers who lose their grip on the chains. The were-eagle begins to demolish the room, not even sparing the antique furniture. The chains on its legs flail about striking Natasha, then Rafe, then Kip. The only gun with ammo scuttles across the floor out of sight. The beast grows more confident with its wings.

It looks for the door.

Marcy, "Don't let it get out! Don't let it escape the room! We must keep it in the Abbey!"

The beast makes for the door. Rafe grabs a chain but can't hold it. His grip strength just won't do against this monster. Marcy looks for the gun. She sees it and lunges for it.

Trevor, still wearing chains himself, takes hold of one of the flailing manacles. He attaches one end of his own shackles to the loose leg-iron, chaining himself to the chains of the beast. He shouts, "Take hold of me! He can't shake me off now!"

Kip lunges and grabs Trevor as the were-eagle leaves the library entrance.

Out on the Abbey grounds

Johan and a few buddies in brown shirts amuse themselves kicking a hairy-man. The hairy-man cowers at their blows. They hear a commotion towards the library.

The sound comes from the were-eagle, dragging Trevor, chained to a chain on the were-eagle's leg. Trevor works to keep his footing as Kip hangs onto Trevor for dear life. The were-eagle flaps its wings and rises up, kept from flying away only by the weight of men hanging onto its chains.

The flapping wings spread the smell of the beast throughout the Abbey grounds. The wings spread the pheromones all the way back to Johan, who again kicks the hairy-man. Johan gloats, "See how it cringes."

The hairy-man sniffs the air. It twitches. It writhes. It doubles over in agony.

Johan laughs, "I wound it."

The hairy-man transforms into a werewolf; all claws, teeth and rage. It attacks Johan.

Poor Johan.

Within the upper cable car room

Panicked Nazis flood into the cable car. They argue over rank order, elite status, ODESSA privileges, and escape protocol. They disagree on the relevant differences between a Knight Colonel of the Order of Teutonic Acolytes of the Great Resolution verses a Baron Captain Adept of the Grand Gothic Order of the Sacred Relic (Second Class). Consensus fails them. High Teutons of the Nibelungen Reich trample Grand Margraves of the Condor Legion of Thule. The Elect finally pack themselves into the cable car. They scream at the worker to lower it.

Werewolves and weredogs race into the room. They attack the cable car worker, making mincemeat of him. They race into the cable car after the last terrified member of the ODESSA Elect runs into it.

Blood splashes against the cable car windows.

Out on the Abbey grounds

The were-eagle bounds through the grounds. It makes for

the walls of the cloister. In a mighty wing-flapping leap it hoists itself over the cloister walls dragging Trevor and Kip with it. Rafe runs to a cloister entrance and into the cloister in pursuit. Marcy and Natasha close behind.

Marcy, "Natasha! This place is going to blow! We have maybe ten minutes before it all goes up."

Natasha looks about at the walls. She sees the charges set. She runs into the cloister, Marcy hot behind.

The cloister

The were-eagle crosses the cloister, hindered by Trevor and Kip. It heads for the bell tower past the opposite cloister wall. It drags the men holding its chains. Trevor, chained to a chain that is itself chained to the beast, has little choice in where he goes. Kip, with nothing but his arm-strength to keep his grip barely hang on.

Natasha catches up to Rafe. They run alongside each other.

Natasha, "Bombs."

Rafe, "Bombs?"

Natasha, "Everywhere. Soon to explode."

The were-eagle summits the cloister wall knocking Kip off and dragging Trevor over. Exhausted, Rafe stops to pick up Kip.

Rafe, breathing heavy, "Bombs."

Kip, "Uh?"

Rafe, "The latest surprise: bombs. Everywhere. About to go boom."

Natasha races past them out of the cloister. Rafe and Kip stagger after her.

Kip, "What do we do?"

Rafe, "Stop the monster, save Trevor, and shelter at whatever structure looks least worth blowing up." They set out again at a run.

Marcy follows, right on their heels.

The were-eagle drags Trevor to the bell-tower. Natasha grabs Trevor's waist, Rafe leaps to grab Natasha, but the were-eagle shakes off both as it claws and flaps its way slowly up the bell-tower, pulling Trevor up as well. Natasha and Rafe kneel at the bottom of the tower, left behind.

Kip races past the exhausted pair and into the bell-tower itself.

Natasha looks up. She sees an object obscuring her view. A bomb. A gasping Rafe reaches for it.

Natasha, "No."

Rafe stops. Right, do not touch the bomb. He works to catch his breath. He looks up at the ascending were-eagle. He watches as the were-eagle climbs toward the bell tower roof. "Why there?"

Natasha, "Good place to nest?"

Rafe, "Or to launch."

The were-eagle rises. Trevor walks up the side of the building at the end of his chain, keeping pace and slowing the beast down with his weight. He looks like a man ascending a mountain—behind a giant eagle-man-beast.

Within the bell-tower

Kip bounds up the stairs taking them three at a time. He moves with the strength of Hercules. He will not let Trevor down.

Rafe enters the bell-tower and makes a much more fatigued ascent; panting heavily in the thin mountain air. Andean Mountain monster chases are more exhausting than the movies let on. One really needs no less than three weeks acclimatization time. Someone should send a memo.

Kip runs, he does not walk, up the stairs. He can see the top of the bell-tower as he climbs the spiral staircase. The ropes for the bell dangle to the floor below.

Outside the bell-tower, the were-eagle obtains the

opening of the tower below its roof. It rests a moment in one of the four great rectangular openings that let the sound of the bell ring forth. Trevor, in a true feat of strength, pulls himself almost to the foot-claw of the beast. It starts to kick at him and to use its wing-hands to climb to the roof of the tower.

Trevor crawls through the opening into the bell-tower just as a bullet dings off the side of the tower near the beast's head. Below, Trevor sees Natasha with the pistol that Marcy recovered from the library. Natasha steadies her aim with both hands, but the distance and darkness argue against her.

Within the bell-tower, Kip makes the landing where the bell hangs as Trevor pulls himself in.

Trevor, "Grab the fiend's other manacle!"

Kip lunges through the rectangular opening and takes hold of the manacle dangling from the beast. The were-eagle now rests on the roof of the bell tower. It tests its wings for flight.

Kip, "The place will explode."

Trevor, "I've already been briefed on that."

Kip wonders at this for an instant. Trevor got the bomb memo before he did?

Trevor releases the shackle on his own waist. He instructs Kip, "Clip them together, around the stone column." Trevor and Kip clip together the two shackles around the nearest stone upright that supports the roof of the bell-tower. Now they have chained the were-eagle to the bell-tower.

Kip, "What now?"

Trevor, "Abandon ship, old boy."

Best suggestion of the day. Kip runs down the spiral stairs. As he runs, taking the stairs four at a time, he hears the bell clang and sees Trevor repelling down the bell-rope past him.

Rafe too watches Trevor repel past him.

Kip yells to Rafe, "Down!"

You don't need to tell Rafe twice; he didn't much care for *up* as a bell-tower direction in the first place. They arrive at the bottom. Kip in time to see Trevor looking up the bell-rope in amazement.

Trevor, "I didn't crack my skull! I didn't receive a single blow to the head! I managed the entire feat without losing consciousness at all!"

Marcy leans in, "Get out of there!"

And out they get.

Outside the Abbey tool shed

Marcy, Rafe, Natasha, Kip and Trevor rest at the tool shed, a building unadorned with explosives. They look at the bell-tower. The were-eagle struggles against its chains, held fast to the stone post.

The sky lights up as explosions go off. The lab to their left blows up. The library goes up. The cloister. The bell-tower explodes from its base, collapsing inward, bringing down the sounding bell, the tower top, and the screeching were-eagle. All into a crater now formed where once the bell-tower stood. More explosions take out half the church, leaving only the crypt entrance unscathed. Just the explosive finale readers of *The Silencers* have longed for.

Kip pats Trevor on the back, "To think. You were chained to that thing."

Trevor looks at the dust rising from the collapsed bell-tower. He faints.

Out on the lower mountainside – morning

The Silencers and their allies walk from the cave entrance up a gentle hill toward Miriam who waits with Chris. Miriam holds Katrina. Beneath their feet, two hairy-monkey-kids play. What a world.

The Cohens have packed away their guns; farmers again. Hadassah bears the heaviest pack, because no one carries Hadassah's load but Hadassah.

The Silencers walk in pairs. Marcy in the lead, smiling at Chris ahead of her up the hill. Kip and Trevor behind with

Rafe and Natasha bringing up the rear. Joy prevails in the morning sun.

Marcy, "Ahoy!"

Katrina leaps from Miriam to Marcy. Marcy nods thanks to Miriam. Miriam smiles.

Katrina, "Mommy! Mommy! Daddy got werewolves!"

Marcy, "I can see that."

Chris, "I knew you wanted a bigger family."

Katrina, "Can we keep them?"

Marcy, "One monkey is enough." Marcy rubs noses with Katrina, "And I'm sure they have monkey families of their own."

Papa Cohen joins them. He hugs Miriam, nods at Chris and Marcy. He and Miriam walk on.

Chris, "I notice you left quite a mess at the top of the mountain. I try to teach our Little Wrecking Ball to put away her toys and you burn monasteries to the ground in full view."

Marcy, "Extenuating circumstances."

Behind them, Kip and Trevor walk up the hill. Trevor says to Kip, "I think I did rather well there at the end."

Kip, "Are you kidding? You are my hero! The man of the hour! The savior of the day!"

Trevor beams with delight, "Do you really think so? I mean the others did contribute a great deal of course, but do you really think so?"

Kip, "I give you the medal, hands down." They arrive on the hilltop.

Chris, to Kip, "Kip! Good to see you."

Kip, "Chris!"

They hug, old friends together again.

Chris, "And Trevor all in one piece." Chris tugs at a bit of Trevor's disguise. "Still covered in hair."

Kip beams with pride, "The way I put that stuff on. He will be covered in hair for at least—" Kip sees the terror on Trevor's face, "I mean to say. Uh. It will fall out eventually."

Trevor, "*Fall* out? Define *eventually*."

Behind them Rafe and Natasha climb the hill.

Rafe, "*The idiot man?*"

Natasha, "All I could think of on spur of moment."

Rafe, "Thanks, that even makes it worse."

Natasha smiles. Really, she can do that, and this time spontaneously. She says, "Sorry."

Rafe, "You know that I worked it all out. You may have missed that part. Orlok, the silver haired fellow who became a giant monster ... but you know him ... a colleague of yours ... how you do love to hook up with the super-villains ... Anyway, he intended to make werewolves out of werewolves and transplant Hitler's brain into one."

Natasha, "Of course he did."

Rafe, "No really. They saved Hitler's brain."

Natasha, "Of course they did."

Rafe, "Really. I saw it. In a vat. With eyes. Really this time."

Hadassah passes and glances at Natasha. Natasha returns her look. Two Amazons, each having chosen a different path. Hadassah treks on carrying her full pack up and over the hill.

Natasha, to Rafe, "Tell me again how you escaped the clutches of the nefarious Karl."

Rafe, "No Kung fu involved, just a bit of my *idiot man* cunning." They crest the hill and join the others.

Chris, "Rafe? Natasha? What are you two doing here?"

Marcy, "Yes, I'm waiting to be briefed on that myself."

Rafe, "Well, it will interest you to know that I discovered this whole plot deciphering clues left by the fool Halftrain and by Chris himself here."

Chris, "Oh?"

Trevor, "Unlikely."

Rafe pulls from his pocket two papers. He hands one to Marcy and the other to Chris.

Rafe, to Marcy, "Our official briefing."

Marcy looks and listens.

Rafe, "Marcy missing, by way of the sea, taken by the

world's fourth richest man—Orlok I suppose—by way of Palacia. Mentions Doctor Damarung of course." Rafe points at the relevant parts of the paper as he explains, "Nazi asthmatics took longer, but I saw Klaus Attler as the same fellow Chris tracked down, the one who owned the charter company along with Bruer and Hoffman." Rafe considers the tangles in all his discoveries, "Never found Mr. Cargo, but I cracked the completely evil cult wide open." Pause, "I'm still not sure about all that penile restitution business." Long pause. "Anyway, point being, Halftrain and Chris left subtle clues and I followed those to find Marcy and her kidnappers."

Marcy, "No one kidnapped me."

Chris, "I didn't leave any clues."

One despairs of explaining things to people sometimes. Rafe taps the paper in Chris's hands, "Right there. Out to sea facts." Pause. "Or maybe Odessa facts. But all of it right there. From your bulletin board. X marks the spot."

Kip, "XOX"

Rafe, annoyed, "Whatever."

Chris looks at the paper, "X cancels the project. I wrote these notes prior to Marcy coming up with this working vacation." Chris glances at Marcy; Marcy inspects her toes.

Chris, "The Otusia are a cargo cult tribe in the altiplano region of Mauritania in Africa. An interesting study in coevolutionary practices. Attler made first contact in 1934. The rest are references to *The Proceedings of the Society of Cultural Anthropology*."

Natasha, "Volume seven, number three." She smiles nicely at the bollixed Rafe.

Rafe, "No. Wait. *I* did this. Without the clues on Chris's bulletin board no man on earth could have deciphered the mad ravings of Halftrain's briefing. We could never have found you."

Marcy looks at the page, "Standard confusion from Halftrain, but I can make it out." She translates from the page, "Mission: engineer ODESSA Overthrow. Research the

Fourth Reich's manipulation of travel, customs, and duties. ODESSA commander Count Orlok seeks unknown 'Final Resolution' using services of a Dr. Damarung—biomedical engineer. Must stop Dr. Damarung at all cost. Nazis disguised as monks using Kloster Adler in Argentina—seek and find Damarung the biomedical engineer here. The group uses traditional SS escape route through Buenos Aries."

Marcy looks up. She looks at Rafe who looks stunned, like a mackerel just swam in off an Andean Mountain top to slap him in the face with yet another mackerel. Marcy says, "All right there really."

Everyone nods. Plain as day. To one who knows how to read. Natasha gives Rafe a little pat on the shoulder, next time soldier.

Rafe, "Wait. I need an explanation. If no one kidnapped you, how do you come to be here? If no one kidnapped you, how did *I* come to be here? How did Kip and Trevor come to be here? How did we all get here at the same time? I need to be re-briefed."

Trevor, "Oh, please. For the love of God and all his children, I beg you, I implore you, for the sake of my aching head: no more briefings!"

Marcy takes Trevor by the arm, "Come on Trevor. I'll buy you a drink. And I promise, no one will explain anything to anyone."

And so we step away from this happy group, making their way, chatting amicably. Katrina and monkey-boys playing at their feet; a pub and a drink ahead, the smoking ruins of the Kloster Adler behind.

Within a storeroom at the Cohen farm – night

Outside, the wind blows. The sound presses against the windows. Inside, dimly lit, we see our way through a virtual shrine to Judaism; an ode in objects to Israel and its people. On a table: Jewish scripture, a Menorah with candles burning, a shofar on a small pedestal. Above the table a large flag of Israel. To one side a framed picture of David Ben-Gurion, on the other a framed picture of Golda Meir. Along the walls hang pictures of Moshe Dayan, kibbutz farmers, Ehud and Ezra during their military service, and Hadassah cleaning her rifle.

As we approach the far wall we see the broad back of Papa Cohen, bent over reading. He reads from a well bound book. He reads in German. Papa Cohen reads, "And God gave these laws to the people, for everyone to hold dear in the heart and follow all the days of their lives."

He closes the book.

Papa Cohen, "That will be enough Torah reading for tonight. I am sure you got very much out of it, yes?"

Para Cohen rises and retrieves a small lectern. He puts it in front of him and places the book on the lectern, open.

Papa Cohen, "I will leave the book open for you to read. Tomorrow I will read you more from the Torah." Papa Cohen speaks as if to a small child, "Or perhaps we will again read of how the Israelites came to the Promised Land."

Stepping back, we see to whom he addresses these remarks. We see a vat, filled with fluid. In the vat floats a brain, eyes included, looking ahead. Papa Cohen rolls a small television into view of the eyes. He says, "And for the rest of the night you will watch a television show: *Building a Better Israel*." He turns on the television: inspirational Israeli State TV. Papa Cohen says, "So many happy people!"

Papa Cohen leaves the room, closing the door.

By the blue flicker of Israeli farmers we look to the television, to the book open on Exodus, to the brain in the vat unable to close its eyes.

A benefit to the soul? A subtle form of torture? Works either way.

ABOUT THE AUTHOR

Whip Lipsey

Whip Lipsey grew up in Georgia, came of age in Missouri, and dropped out of high school in California. He holds a bachelor's degree in history from the University of California at Irvine and a PhD in philosophy from the University of Rochester. He left academia to work as a screenwriter (and was shocked to learn that writing for Hollywood does not require a doctorate). After twenty years raising his three children as a full-time father, he has returned to writing.